Darlene Hawes has been writing short stories since retiring from her psychological counselling career in 2017. Her first book, *Manifesting Memories,* was published in 2023 and was well-received. A mother of three adult sons and grandmother to six children, Darlene enjoys participating in family events and activities, in addition to listening to music and escaping to her muse. Darlene resides in Halifax, Nova Scotia.

This work is dedicated to those courageous souls whose struggles have led them inward to discover, accept, and know themselves through the mastery of their egos. To those with humility and strength to face their shadows; a most difficult journey, enabling them to contribute to the betterment of our world. You are my heroes.

Darlene Hawes

IT IS IN YOU

AUSTIN MACAULEY PUBLISHERS®

LONDON * CAMBRIDGE * NEW YORK * SHARJAH

Ordering Information
Quantity sales: Special discounts are available on quantity purchases by corporations, associations, and others. For details, contact the publisher at the address below.

Publisher's Cataloging-in-Publication data
Hawes, Darlene
It Is in You

ISBN 9798891556195 (Paperback)
ISBN 9798891556201 (ePub e-book)

Library of Congress Control Number: 2024911736

www.austinmacauley.com/us

First Published 2024
Austin Macauley Publishers LLC
40 Wall Street, 33rd Floor, Suite 3302
New York, NY 10005
USA

mail-usa@austinmacauley.com
+1 (646) 5125767

I am sincerely grateful to my dear friends David and Carmel Edison, Faye Hawes and Donna Ward for their grammatical and editing skills and for their ongoing support and encouragement of my work. Special thanks to Angela Jacquard (posthumously). Dianna Lim, Ron Corbett and Terry Lewin for reading some of the stories and providing considered and helpful feedback. To Austin Macauly Publishers for their patience, cooperation and belief in me as an author and for helping me share my stories with others, thank you.

Table of Contents

Preface

Our everyday communications and expressions are often lines in songs. Things like 'what doesn't kill you makes you stronger', a line I've heard all my life, but never had sung to me. Or, perhaps, 'anything you want, you've got it', said by those who love us and would do anything for us. These expressions are not only stated but now they are easy to sing because Kelly Clarkson and Roy Orbison put music to them. In reality, we are always speaking or writing words that are subsequently put to music.

Some forty years ago when my youngest son would ask me a question, I had the habit of replying to him with a lyrical response. Sometimes it was a line from a song, and other times, I simply sang out my reply. At first, he seemed amused and a little intrigued that I could do this so consistently, until one day, when he was about eight years old, he had enough. He demanded I stop doing that and give him a straight answer. His irritation amused me. I continued, knowing that he didn't care if I sang or spoke the reply as long as he got what he wanted. Sometimes he just grew impatient for a direct answer.

Recently I have caught him doing the same thing; the singing reply. I have observed him doing this with his children when they ask him a question. I've noticed how the moment shifts from boring to fun, how cheerfulness is exemplified in the responder, and how levity is inserted into the situation. Sometimes his children will even sing a line back to him. As an adult though, he has not limited sharing this behavior with his children. Sometimes when I text him, I receive a musical reply. One day he wrote that he had gone shopping for some new clothes. When I asked what he bought, he sent me some lyrics from a song released when he was only three years old that mentioned 'matador boots, iridescent socks with a matching shirt and chinos'. My boy was just keeping the faith! (Billy Joel; Keeping The Faith, 1983). It was payback time and I loved it!

I

This collection of stories is interspersed with musical lines that fit the tale. If you are of a certain age, you may find yourself reminiscing about hunting for Waldo on the cereal box that was plunked on your breakfast table. Only this is not pictorial. You have to read the words to spot the tunes.

Unlike the other stories in this collection, The Boys Who Played Ball is primarily a true story unencumbered by the author's intrigue and imagination. Some characters/players were interviewed and provided their recollections of events, photos and scrapbooks as evidential support to their memories. The scrapbooks contained newspaper clippings from the sports pages of their local papers by the reporters covering the games. Several referenced reports were unanimously and independently corrected by the players themselves. The moment, the field, the play, the score, and other details were etched in the minds of the players. Each time I explained that I got a certain piece of information from their scrapbook articles, I was told, point blank, that it wasn't right. Subsequently, I was given the facts by the players. Experience is usually where truth is found.

Only four players were interviewed for the ball story. The other players, who were still living, either could not be located or were too ill to be interviewed. Hanson and Densmore, the Josey brothers, the coach and captain, who were foundational to the Atoms team both passed away within months of each other and during the writing of this story. While the games and events in the story are as true as memories allow, they are much more. This story resonates with the dedicated sportspeople we have known and the sportsmanship we still witness in the youthful athletes playing today's games, giving their best to their sport and cheered on by delighted fans. Even this story has its musical lines. And it's time for it to be told. 'Don't say it ain't so, you know the time is now' (John Fogerty, Centerfield, 1985).

II

Wake Up the Girls

I sat on the rocking chair, near the edge, so my feet would touch the floor. As my mother lay on the sofa, resting, I could not take my eyes off her. It was so unusual to see her lying down, and I had certainly never seen her lying down early in the morning. She would be busy in the kitchen this time of day, getting things underway and ready for the family. As I watched, she turned her head toward me. "Nene," she said, to ensure she had my attention, although my focus was already on her. "Go tell the girls to get up."

It was an eerie feeling and a sense of obedience that carried me quickly up the stairs to awaken my sisters. That word, "go," had an urgency about it. As I shook the girls, who shrugged me off, I yelled to them, "You have to get up now, Mama said!" Something in me was insistent on getting me back downstairs with my mother. I returned to the rocking chair on a strangely quiet Saturday morning and continued watching her. Mama opened her eyes. Seeing me there, still looking at her, she may have thought I had disobeyed her. This time she spoke with a firmness I recognized but in a weaker-sounding voice: "Go, wake up the girls."

I jumped to my feet and headed up the steps. With a frightened panic sounding in my voice, I replied, "I already told them, but I'll tell them again!" The youngest of my sisters took notice of the concern in me when I shook her again. I said, "Something's wrong! Mama's lying down! She said you gotta get up!" My sister's eyes opened and, as they met mine, I knew my words had registered with her. I ran back downstairs, pulled by some need to be there.

I resumed my perch. Suddenly there was a terribly offensive smell in the room. Mama didn't seem to notice it. What I didn't notice was that a massive stroke had stolen her away; taken her into a coma. I, also, had no way of knowing that the last words I would ever hear her speak were: "Go, wake up the girls." Nor did I know the unconscious impact those words would have on my life.

Within moments, everything seemed to get busy and whispery, yet life seemed to be in slow motion at the same time. Daddy had returned from the barn, where he had been tending to the animals, just as my sister came downstairs. Another sister appeared, phone calls were being made, voices were hushed, and there was a strange calm; not a peaceful calm, but the kind that's filled with fear. My sister directed me out of there when Daddy was on the phone. The rocking chair was near the phone that hung on the wall, and I imagine, I was not to hear what was being said. She was sixteen and quietly taking charge, but I could tell she was scared, too. Any minutiae that filled the morning faded with the arrival of my uncle, Mama's brother, in his van. Again, my attention was redirected away from the activities about to take place.

The next thing I remember was looking out the window as the van went down our driveway with my parents and uncle inside. I was told they had to take Mama to the hospital. A lapse of time is part of the blur that disturbed the clarity for much of the remainder of the day. Only two events remained clear. One was that Daddy returned home without Mama; the other was that the milk needed to be strained.

Mama had let me help strain the milk before, but I had never seen that stainless steel, two-gallon bucket that full. I said to my sister, "It's so full! How did he carry it from the barn without spilling it?" She told me to just leave it as it was too heavy for me to strain. I told her I thought I could do it. Before Yoda or Nike put it in the mainstream, it was in my blood. It was not a moment of trying; it was a moment of just doing it right. While everyone else was active getting food ready, cleaning up, and helping the kitchen feel more like a Saturday morning, I went about my business. I got out the large bowl and cloth Mama used when straining the milk. This was all rural people did for 'pasteurization' in those days. No one was ever sick. Dairy, like most food products, was usually produced and consumed daily. There were no 'best before' dates needed. It was best if you got it before someone else did, or you'd have to wait until tomorrow.

First of all, I decided I would ladle a few cups of milk out of the bucket and put it in the metal basin where Mama sometimes kept cream. I wrapped that cloth tightly around the top of the bucket and held on to it near the sides of the handle as I had done once or twice under Mama's watchful eyes. I had the bucket near the edge of the table and pressed against my chest for support. Before I lifted it to pour, I looked up and caught my sister's glance. She was probably just being 'on the ready' in case there was a disaster. I figured if I could just get that first quart strained into the bowl, I would pour those cups of milk back into the bucket and strain it. It would be easier because the bucket would be lighter. I did it successfully, and didn't spill a drop! I knew Mama would be proud of me. But now, it was time for me to be proud of myself. There comes a time when we need to acknowledge our own accomplishments and not expect or wait for it from someone else. It felt like that moment had arrived. As I took the bucket and cloth to the sink for cleaning, my sister commented that I did a good job. A confirmation of what I knew.

More than thirty years later, my sister and I found ourselves talking about that day. In our conversation, I remarked about straining the milk when her husband laughed and said, "You wouldn't have strained the milk. You were only nine years old. You wouldn't have been able to lift a bucket full of milk!"

I smiled at him and said, "Don't know if I could do it today, but I did it that day!" At the same time, I felt a line being drawn inside me. No, not drawn! Deeply carved inside me by my experiences. I knew it was a line that I must never let anyone cross if they are trying to take from me my experiences. My experiences are part of me. I've endured them; I have suffered through them; I have been joyful because of them; and I have brought all my attention and all my senses to them. They are mine! No one else gets to deny them or rewrite them.

How dare anyone tell another that what they have lived through and processed didn't happen, just because they can't or won't believe it? It is more than an assault on one's integrity; it is an assault on one's identity. I wasn't angry with my brother-in-law for his reasoning ability or his limited justification for why it would be impossible for me to lift the milk bucket. As my sister searched her memory, she looked at us and said, "I remember something about you straining the milk." Yet her husband insisted it couldn't have happened because his sister's little girl, who was nine, would never be able to lift a heavy bucket of milk like that. His reasoning seemed sure, his comparison adequate, and he voiced his opinion with certainty.

However, he was wrong about me. Another thirty years have passed, and my youngest granddaughter is now nine. When the older ones were nine, I could have said the same thing about them at that age. Each one of them has the keen ability to assess whether or not they can do something. Once they decide they can, they have no doubt, and they have the strength and determination to follow through successfully with their undertakings. I have witnessed it in each one of them. There is no point in making those slotted comparisons with others by age or size. Those are not the things that make the difference. They only categorize people as being the same because they share a couple of attributes. It serves to encourage a herd mentality and not recognize the individual. What makes the difference is discovering for ourselves what we are made of! We can all join in the run for the roses if we discover, and remember that we have in us that which will drive us and bring us home.

It's important to realize there are only two ways we can 'wake up' someone else. Either we have to awaken ourselves or we have to snore so loudly that we disturb someone else's slumber, then they are very apt to wake us up, too! You see, if we are awake or conscious, we can help others come into awareness. Yet, if we are so unconscious, our behavior may be very disturbing to others, and that could enable them to be mindful of their own awareness. They may walk away and leave us to our snoring, or they may try to shake us out of it. Sometimes we are even awakened by our own snoring.

When we become fully awake and aware, no longer wanting to snore or pull that blanket over our heads, the energy we give off to those in our presence will be noticed by them. Our energy will vibrate at a higher frequency and will attract similar vibrations. If we are awake, we will know when we resonate with someone who is on our frequency.

My mother's last words never formed a conscious belief in me that it was my duty in life to 'go wake up the girls.' But as I look back and reflect on my life, I have found that I have spent many years 'waking up the girls.' In the process, I have also been awakened to many things a girl needs to know. Whether in friendships or career, I have learned that my own awakenings have been helpful in bringing awareness to others. There have been times when others have had to shake me out of my snoring and wake me up. Sometimes I have only been willing to change my position to sleep more quietly because I haven't been fully awakened on some matters. It's a step in the right direction. It's important to try to keep moving in the right direction.

There will be times when an experience will help us see something clearly and gain understanding, but most often, we tend to wake up gradually. And we all know people who refuse to wake up, no matter how much we shake them or how much noise we or they make. In these cases, I have found it is better to just let them sleep until they are ready to wake; otherwise, they'll keep you busy all day long just trying to wake them. But your life and awareness are important, too. Part of my own awakening has been to realize that not everyone who needs to wake up wants to wake up.

In high school, I recall going for walks with a couple of friends. These girls were quite talkative and often said things without much thought or reflection. One day, they were once again chatting about how much their mothers 'got on their nerves,' and what they were required to do at home, and how they could predict what their mothers would have to say about something. Whether it was my inability to participate in the conversation, or my annoyance with how critical they sounded, I only briefly weighed my comment before I spoke. During a break in the chatter, I said, "You both should be very thankful you have a mother to complain about."

What followed was an awkward, hundred-yard silence. I think I did wake up those girls. We hung out together for the rest of our high school years, and I never again heard them speak with disregard for their mothers. Sometimes we just need to be reminded of our blessings.

Ellen, a friend of mine from university, reappeared in my life a few years ago. I was very happy to see her. She was working in a local retail outlet, and we chatted and got caught up on each other's news. She told me she was married and had a teenage daughter. We said we would stay in touch, but we didn't. It was another five years before I saw her again. I learned she was recently divorced. This time, we exchanged phone numbers. Later, I called and invited her to attend a Christmas gathering I was having at home. Ellen would know a couple of the other guests.

In our first few encounters during our reacquaintance, I noticed she spoke almost entirely about her ex-husband and the divorce. I assumed it was early in her process, and she was just a little preoccupied with the details. She said she had been in therapy since the divorce. One day I suggested we go for lunch to enjoy ourselves, and she could forget about the ex for a while. Ellen sounded eager to do that, but during lunch, there was no topic she could not turn into an association with him, including how crispy and delicious the salad was. That, too, was a reminder of how he once complained about a meal that was not fresh enough for him. I began having second thoughts about spending any more time with her.

Life itself tends to bring us enough challenges and hardships. It seems like a bad choice for us to seek out unpleasant experiences and spend any part of our lives in those if we don't have to. A few weeks later, she called me to go for coffee with her. We met at a nearby coffee shop and spent well over an hour in conversation about her 'miserable' ex. I asked Ellen if she was happy to have him out of her life. She assured me she was. I suggested that she keep him out of her life by not allowing him into her thoughts and conversations all the time. I thought that since five years had passed, her ex had probably moved on with his life, and she might want to do the same. She said she has been seeing a therapist once a month for the past five years, and she still can't get over what her ex did to her and that she will never forgive him. As I listened, I quickly did the math, and thought, *That's sixty sessions of this, and she continues to talk about him to anyone who will listen.*

She finished up with, "I'll gladly burn in hell before I'll ever forgive him!"

I simply replied, "Forgiveness is for you, not him."

That comment did not land well. What followed was a robust outburst as Ellen pushed her chair away from the table and exclaimed, "Now that's a statement I could never understand." She had obviously been told that, based on her religious teachings and numerous other beliefs she held, yet she could make no sense of how forgiving his faults and weaknesses could help her in any way. He needed to be punished! What Ellen could not see was that she was punishing herself with all her ruminating and negativity. It was at that moment that she woke me up. Could it be possible that in sixty years she had never forgiven anyone and experienced a release and sense of peace from it? I sensed she and I would never be on the same page in this lifetime. I knew, at that moment, that I was not prepared to put any more energy into a relationship with her. Our experiences, our life situations, and how we interpreted them meant there was no common ground on which we could build a balanced friendship.

I was about to do to her the same thing that he had done. She had already told me it was something she could never forgive: walking away because I, too, had enough. I was not willing to be in any kind of relationship that left me feeling exhausted and depressed. It did not nurture me. I found it a challenge over the next year to ignore her calls, messages, and invitations. But I knew I could not allow myself to be pulled into her negative neediness again. I knew from psychology that intermittent reinforcement would only continue her behavior. I could not reply to her now and then. It had to be 'cold turkey.' I would no longer respond. My job was to deal with all those judgmental voices within me that said, 'bad friend; unkind person; she needs your help; she needs someone.' I knew better than to be tricked by false guilt; it was my responsibility to myself to act on what I knew to be true. We have to take care of ourselves too. I wish my mother had taken better care of herself and not just everyone else. Maybe, in an unconscious way, that was one of the things she realized girls needed to be awakened to: the importance of taking care of themselves.

It has been well over a year since Ellen and I have spoken. Recently on Facebook, of all places, she posted that on that particular day, twenty-one years ago, she and her husband exchanged marriage vows, and on that same day, fifteen years later, he announced he wanted a divorce… I stopped reading. I deleted the message. It wasn't that she destroyed our friendship with her negativity; it was that I needed to wake up to my own behaviors of being drawn into nurturing others when they could never be satiated. She seemed comfortably stuck in a place of victimhood. I was grateful for our reconnection and I felt she was a blessing to me; an angel sent to wake me up. I found myself trying to get her to open her eyes, but it was she who opened mine. We all need each other to help us wake up.

There is a great deal of grief that life will bring. We need to find a way to release it or it will build up in us. When grief arrives, we need to realize it needs the very same things we do. It needs to be embraced, loved, satisfied, and released. If we are respectful of it, grief will be respectful of us. Sometimes we deny it, and it will hang around like the plague. This was the case with an eighty-year-old woman who came to see me.

Her family physician, whose office was across the hall from mine, knocked on my door one day wanting a word with me. He wanted to refer one of his patients and asked if I could see her very soon. This was not his first referral to me but it was the first time he had made such a personal and urgent request on behalf of a patient. His patient called the next morning and I arranged to see her the following day. She arrived with her husband, and he asked if they could both attend the session. I said that was up to his wife. After completing the usual and necessary protocols, I was told that the referral was because she had been diagnosed with cancer, and she just wanted someone else to talk to besides her husband. At least that is what she was offering in front of him. He was studying me intently and would cast nervous glances toward her when she spoke. I realized this meeting was an assessment of me and whether or not they felt I could be trusted and compassionate enough for what needed to be shared.

Near the end of the session, the wife asked if she could come back and see me again. We made an appointment for the following week, and I told her she could come alone, as I sensed she needed that to be said. I also added that they could attend together if she preferred and, if her husband would like to have a session alone, we could also set that up as well. He insisted that he didn't need to talk to me and that he was only there to support her. She had told her doctor she wanted to talk to somebody else. They arrived together for the second session, but before sitting down, she shoved him toward the door and told him to go. He asked if she was sure about that, and she insisted he leave. He glanced at me, and I smiled and said I would take good care of her. They both laughed, and he left. I did not know the source of his anxiety, but I did know they were married in their late teens, had a daughter who lived an hour's drive away, and they shared a devotion to one another.

She was only seated for a few minutes when she asked if it would be alright if she laid down. I told her to make herself comfortable. She adjusted a cushion behind her head as she curled up on the sofa she and her husband sat on during the last session. She was ready to talk.

The matters of aging, cancer, and one's eventual demise were not of much concern to her. She accepted these things as part of life. She reflected that her life had been pretty good. She said that she and her family had been churchgoers, but circumstances in life had changed that over the years. Her big concern, what she really wanted to talk about was, as she put it, 'going to meet my maker'. She shared the burden, the guilt, and the heartache she had carried for over fifty years.

She and her husband had two children. One day, after her husband left for work, she was in the house with the children. The older child, their son, ran outside and went out on the street. A car hit him, and he died. She always blamed herself for his death. She was concerned that her God would find her guilty, too. As I listened, she reviewed all her thoughts about what she might have done to prevent that moment. All the 'if onlys' she could imagine telling herself might have changed it all. The pain was so overwhelming that even her husband could not deal with the loss and how she was suffering, so he refused to talk about it. It was a subject they never spoke of again. They had agreed that they needed to get on with life. They had another child to raise, and they immersed themselves in her, in work and in community activities. She said she was always able to present a good face and show strength around others. As she was nearing the end of her life, her only concern was facing God and the possibility that he might condemn her.

All those years she blamed herself for something that was not her fault. There was no way she could have known what the next moment would hold, or how her entire life would change because of that unpredictable moment. Something in her must have known the truth. She needed an affirmation of her innocence. She needed that from someone she felt she could really believe; someone she felt wasn't just trying to console her. She needed to hear it from an independent stranger she felt she could trust. She needed to be empowered to release her self-blame. The condemnation of herself was her own doing, not her Gods. Love is always waiting to welcome us back to our innocence.

There seems to be a need for us to be awakened to our willingness to occasionally take on burdens and guilt that are not our own. There are consequences to ourselves for our beliefs. It is important for each one of us to take responsibility for our thoughts, words, and deeds, to make the necessary changes, and to forgive ourselves and others. It allows us to wake up, grow up, move forward, and be wiser. It is a real detriment to our well-being; to our mental, physical, emotional, and spiritual selves to hold on to and not release our vexations. The propensity for us to become agents of cause, when we are not, is something to be aware of for it holds a hubris that is false and always in conflict with our truth. It is a barrier we erect between ourselves and our God, our higher self.

My client said she felt much better after her session, but added she would like to make one more appointment. It was arranged. The following week she did not show up for her appointment. She may not have been feeling well, or she may have forgotten. Either way, I called with a reminder and left a message with a date and time to reschedule. I did not hear back until the day of the next scheduled appointment. Her husband called to say his wife had passed away the previous week. It was only then I fully realized the meaning of the anxiety and the urgency.

They and the doctor all knew what I was not told: She would not live much longer. The cancer was advanced and aggressive, and there was no treatment to help her. She had something she urgently needed to address. Her husband didn't want to leave her side. He knew how precious every moment near her was to him. She knew how important it was to release and be freed from her feelings of guilt. At last, she would rest in peace.

There are so many things we need to wake up to if we do not want to immerse our lives in unnecessary pain and struggle. Waking up often means we will need to confront our irrational fears. There is help available. But with or without help, it takes courage to even attempt to overcome a great fear. You must have hope and believe in the possibility that you can overcome it; that you can make a change. It does not matter what the fear is. Fear is equally frightening to the ones held in its grip. Something that fills me with joy is to see the transformation and confidence in someone who has overcome a debilitating fear. Such is truly a witnessing of a resurrection!

My first, and one of my few overwhelming fears, provided me with an understanding of what's possible as I overcame my fear. It was the day after my mother was brought back to our home for her wake.

It was late in the afternoon when her remains were brought to the house. I recall making myself scarce, keeping occupied, and staying away from everyone as much as I could when I saw the hearse coming up the driveway.

I recalled that just a week earlier, my sixteen-year-old sister had taken me and my two youngest brothers to the hospital to see Mama. Her bed was high and we could barely reach to give her a kiss. We were not accustomed to her lack of response, and we weren't there very long. I didn't realize it, at the time, but the visit was probably intended for us to say goodbye to her forever. When I said 'bye', I put my hand in her left hand and I felt her squeeze it. After we left the room, my sister answered something that my youngest, seven-year-old brother asked her. It seemed he was wondering why Mama didn't talk to us. My sister said that maybe Mama didn't know we were there. I very happily and innocently volunteered, "Well, Mama squeezed my hand!"

My sister exclaimed, "What?" I repeated what I said. That was it. The week went by and thirty-seven days after she told me to go wake up the girls, the hospital called to say she had died.

Although I was hiding out, I was working hard at trying to be brave. While everyone else had gone into the living room that evening to witness that the unbelievable was real, I escaped to my bedroom where I tried talking to myself. The next morning, I went and stood in front of the hall mirror to brush my hair. From there, I could also see through the glass of the French door which was beside the mirror. I could see her lying in the coffin at the far end of the living room. My dad, who was coming down the stairs, noticed what I was doing. He asked, "Have you been in to see Mama yet?" I shook my head, no. He saw the fear on my face as he came near me and told me I had to go into the room and see her.

I pulled away as I started to cry and said, "No, I can't."

He put his arm around me and said, "You have to. Come on. I'll go in with you right now." He opened the door and guided my resistant self into the room. When we got to the coffin, he said we could kneel and say some prayers. We did. As I looked at her, I saw a beautiful manikin that looked just like my mother. Praying there beside her was like praying before the statue of the Blessed Virgin Mary at the church. I was no longer afraid. During the hospital visit, I was aware that Mama was aware of me. But she was not aware of me in the living room. My awareness told me she was not there.

In this part of my awakening, there were two important lessons for me. I learned that with love and support and someone to guide us, we can face and overcome our fears. It would be years later when I had more information, that another significant lesson would be learned from these events. It was when my sister asked me if I really felt Mama squeeze my hand that day. I repeated my experience. It was all I knew to tell her. She then told me something. She said that a few days before we were there, she had gone in to see Mama, and Mama squeezed her hand too. She said she told Dad and he talked to the doctor about it. Dad was told that couldn't happen because the stroke had done too much damage.

My sister was left feeling that she could not trust her experience, and was left wondering if she had imagined it. Self-doubting. She also told me that afterward she went and told Dad what I had said. Again, Dad spoke to the doctor and was told of the impossibility of that squeeze happening, but the doctor suggested that since two children experienced it independently, it might just have been a reflex. My second lesson was to never let anyone overrule my experience with their opinions. The doctor, not knowing the reality of my experience, or my sister's, was willing to make a professional declaration that was nothing more than bullshit. I don't know who believed him, but I didn't. What I am sure about is that he didn't know or understand what our mother was made of.

The more we learn to trust ourselves and the truth of our experiences, the easier it becomes to discern truth from untruth. This discernment is essential for girls, especially young girls today.

These days, there are a lot of communication and relationship connections that do not occur in person. Often we do not get to use all the sensory information that is available to us. At one time, we met, saw, and talked to one another in person. We looked into people's eyes and heard their voices. We were often able to detect clues we needed to notice in people, from our sensory information. We didn't have to simply rely on what they wrote to us. Truthful people and skilled liars can write very much the same way. But their eyes, their voices, and their body inflections will only synchronize with truth. Energy does not lie.

When we believe something or have a belief about something external to us, it is not the same as trusting our intuition. If we have an intuitive moment or flash, a sense or feeling, and then ignore the intuition, it does not mean we caused an event or that we could have prevented an event. What it means is that our higher self is speaking to us. We need to wake up and learn to trust our instincts because that is likely how we will be given clues. We must also forgive ourselves for not paying attention to them. Hopefully, that doesn't happen but it might be the wake-up call that reminds us that our higher self was speaking to us in that moment.

Relationships for many girls today are started through Facebook, tweets, Instagram, texting, or sexting as some refer to their communications. I find it incredible since most of us wouldn't choose a pet while wearing a blindfold and earplugs!

Many girls are careful and attentive and their sensibilities notice the words being typed to them. Some are not as aware and need to wake up. A lot of young people have and still do take risks, most of it for fun or experimentation. But taking risks and dabbling in danger seems more destructive and harmful to young girls today than ever before. The obscurity provided through technology allows for deceit, misrepresentation, and being used as an object by predators.

Girls! Wake up to the fact that each one of you is not only a unique and precious soul, but you are also both a student and a teacher. You must learn about yourself because all your thoughts, words, and actions are teaching others how to treat you. For safety's sake, be awake, be aware, and trust your inner wisdom and energy. Your longings and desires could be enough to allow yourself to be deceived by the predators. You need your wits about you; you need to be awake so you do not become someone's prey. You must know and trust yourself, and remember who you really belong to. Not all 'opportunities' are worth taking. Wake up to discernment. Of course, it is the most vulnerable who are preyed upon, and many cannot protect themselves. But always try to stay awake to who you are and stay connected to that which resides within you. It is your salvation. The wake-up call to our own instincts and inner knowing is imperative!

Prevention may be our best medicine. But we cannot prevent what we are not aware of or awakened to. We all need to wake up and become aware of our primary need to prevent harm to ourselves. If you have a flash of doubt about something, then trust that it came to you for a reason. Believe in you!

For those who are awake, know that there are others who will notice your awareness. You may serve as their example and stir in them their desire to allow what is already inside them to flourish. Nobody gave the tin man, or anyone else, something they didn't already have! But they may need encouragement to bring it forth.

We Are the Music

My oldest brother, Wallace, asked me, "Is there a time in the hall tonight?" I smiled and assured him there was. He said he might go. He asked, "You goin?"

I answered, "Oh yes. I'll be there!" I left his house, but the smile remained on my face as I considered that he had called the Saturday night dance 'a time'. Maybe it was so surprising to me because I knew what he meant. Although we are siblings, we were born nearly twenty-three years apart. I thought he spoke more like someone from our father's generation. Nevertheless, a dance by any other name is still a good 'time'!

Our family loved music and dancing. But we were not considered a musical family. There were no lessons taken or performances given. If anyone asked, What do you play? we probably would have answered the radio. Yet, there was always music in our home. There was even such an urge for it that one sister bought a piano, one brother bought a guitar, and another bought a set of drums. Each one of them taught themselves to play those instruments. I recall the girls gathering around the piano for a sing-song over the Christmas holidays as my sister, Lois, played out the Christmas tunes she had taught herself.

As soon as my brother Orrin was working and receiving a pay check, he bought himself a guitar. I never saw him in the house that he didn't have his arms wrapped around that guitar. He even taught another younger brother how to play some chords and pick out a few country tunes. Another brother invested in a set of drums and was seconded into a local band of musicians who played at the Saturday night dances. When he was at home, he taught himself to play those drums and keep time with the beats in the music. He's over seventy years old now, owns three sets of drums, and plays them daily for his relaxation. Without being musicians, music was an integral part of our lives.

The Saturday night dance was the culmination of the week. The dance hall usually held a big crowd that met, but did not exceed, the fire department restrictions. Sometimes there were dances held at church halls or at other venues in the nearby communities but it seemed to me, our community hall always had the best dances and biggest crowds. If one of the other communities held a dance on the same Saturday night, there was just a little more room to dance on the dance floor at our hall.

In the 1950s that hall didn't exist, but there were other local dance halls. In our community, there was the Palace of Fun, once called Temperance Hall, where the young people congregated to dance or watch films. It was just a medium-size wooden structure, and there was nothing palatial about it except the fun. Good times were had there by the local youth and adults. In those days, I think our folks were more like Texans, according to the musical group, Alabama; if you were going to play at our dance halls, you better have a fiddle!

Fortunately, for the locals, there were the Boutilier Brothers who were terrific fiddle and banjo players. They shared their bluegrass sound and talents with their neighbors in that place where the wild roses grow. By the time I was old enough to go to one of the dances where they were playing, they were getting ready to retire from the circuit. I only heard them play once, and it was heart-warming.

There were also records. Recorded music on vinyl: 78s, 45s, and LPs brought the musical hits to the dance halls for sock hops and dances when live music was unattainable. Yet, it always seemed to feel more personal, like there was a bonding of the community members when there were human musicians on the stage singing their hearts and souls out for us and sharing the musical talents they'd been practicing all week. But vinyl turned to high volume could keep the younger crowd on the dance floor. Dancing was a joyful release.

The concrete dance floors in the halls were usually given a sprinkling of Dustbane which the dancers got on their shoes and helped spread it lightly across the dance floor providing enough of a slippery surface for the dancers to glide and turn on smoothly making everyone feel like they were born for these moves. Some called it dance wax. But too much of it could be as dangerous as black ice. The older folks, especially, wouldn't dance then. If any artistic direction was given to the dances, it would have been in the application of Dustbane. It was a very rare Saturday night when there was too much or too little applied.

When I was about twelve, I went to my first official dance. A dance was being held in the Tangier fire hall following the Anglican Church picnic. When it came to picnics and dances, everyone supported one another, and religion, or any other division, was overlooked. I had never been to a real dance before, but I had heard my sisters talk about them. I wanted so much to go so I asked my older sister if I could go with her and her boyfriend. She told me, no. It would be too late for me and I had to be up early to go to morning Mass. I was disappointed. That night I went to bed about nine o'clock. The next thing I knew my sister was rousing me from my slumber asking if I still wanted to go to the dance. I asked what time it was and she told me ten o'clock.

I said, "By the time I get ready and we get there, it will be too late."

She said, "No, it won't. Hurry and get ready right now. We came back home to get you." Bewildered, I stumbled to the bathroom to freshen up. I asked her what I should wear to a dance as I had no time to think about it. She told me to just wear a pair of pants, and a top and brush my hair and I'd be fine. I did as instructed, but worried I might fall back to sleep on the ten-minute drive to the dance. I didn't. I sat in the backseat of her boyfriend's car and told myself to be thankful because they were so kind to come back home and get me.

When we got there and walked into the hall, I was unimpressed. There were only about thirty people there, and there was no band. The music was played on records. Although it was good, popular music, loud and clear, it might have been the reason for so few people being there. The older people still preferred dancing to live bands, not that there were any dead bands we knew of. The Grateful

Dead hadn't even come on the scene yet. Many people felt they could play this kind of music on their phonographs or record players at home; there was no need to go to the dance hall for it. They wanted the real thing, and maybe the 'reel' thing, if they were going out dancing. But here I was at my first dance thinking, *Is that all there is to a dance?* The song hadn't been written yet, but at least Peggy Lee would conclude that we should keep dancing.

We were just standing inside the door of the hall when a very tall boy named Johnny came over to talk with us. Soon I heard the next record play. It was a big hit by The Four Seasons called Rag Doll. Johnny asked me to dance. As I said, he was very tall. I wasn't. He pulled me close to him and said, "You're my little rag doll!" Somewhat naive and unfamiliar with 'pick-up' lines, I had no idea he may be trying to be 'sweet'. I just thought he was plain stupid! It sounded like an insult to me, and I didn't get out of bed for this!

My mind quickly reviewed my look. Although most of my clothes were 'hand-me-downs', the particular outfit I was wearing was not. I thought my hair looked okay, and my sister said it did. I didn't have time to put it up, but I brushed it well. I even considered I might be dancing too floppy because I was still sleepy so I held on to him tightly and stiffened up my body; not great for dancing but only for feeling less like a rag doll. I didn't like having to do this self-scrutiny and I felt myself now holding a grudge. It couldn't have been horrible for him because he asked me for the next dance, a jive, and we got through it alright. At least I wasn't close enough to him to hear any insults. After that dance, I asked my sister, "When can we go home?" I was back in my bed before eleven fifteen.

It was a couple of years later when another of my older sisters and her husband stopped by the house on a Saturday afternoon to ask if I'd like to go to the Legion dance with them that evening. Actually, it was my brother-in-law who asked me. He said Johnny was going with them and I could come along if I wanted to. This time I was wide awake. I could clearly see this scenario unfolding. I politely said, "No, thank you." He insisted for a bit but was careful not to overdo it. He told me if I changed my mind, just give them a call before six and they'd pick me up. I nodded with no intention of phoning them.

Apparently, Johnny was his friend, too. I was silent, but my thoughts said, *No one calls me a rag doll and gets a redo.* What was this Johnny boy thinking? Perhaps he wondered if I had tightened up or loosened up in the past couple of years. As far as I was concerned, his fate had been determined. It would be a few years later before Brenda Lee would release her hit song which would express the sentiments I was feeling that afternoon. In my mind, this guy was Johnny One Time (1969). He had his chance.

When Dolly finished 'slow dancing with the moon' when she was fifteen or so, I believe I became the moon's new dance partner unless he was two-timing on me. I know Conway Twitty didn't think the moon knew anything about love. But I wasn't looking for love; just a dance partner. By 1966, I was dancing with real boys at real dances where bands played and sang all my favorite songs.

Rock 'n' roll had grown popular and could definitely deliver a good time with Elvis Presley's Jailhouse Rock or

Jimmy Rodgers' Honeycomb compelling young and old alike to bring their moves to the dance floor. Sometimes the bands would slip in the occasional pop song and crossover tunes from country and pop music, such as Act Naturally. This tune was sung by both Buck Owens and Ringo Starr and for that matter, everyone on the Eastern Shore and at the local dances. The British Invasion groups were especially enjoyed by the teenagers of the 1960s but that music never drew the eclectic crowds to the dance floors like the tunes of Johnny Cash, Marty Robbins, Hank Williams Senior, or Tom T. Hall (a family favorite because he was a storyteller). Later on, it was Charley Pride and Willy Nelson (singing his own songs) that stole our hearts. A great entertainer himself, George Jones, asked the question, but we still don't know the answer to who will fill their shoes.

Well, some of the young locals gave it a good shot, although none of them became international stars. They certainly shared their musical talents with the community and brought a lot of joy. Some even wrote their own songs and recorded them for local consumption. Those guys were country when it was and wasn't cool! The Don Messer show on television made everyone feel connected musically. Even the newer, local bands, like the one my brother played in, the Country Balladiers, knew it was wise to have in their repertoire of songs some reels, and polkas that got the crowd circling around the dance floor. If there weren't enough men to go around, the women got up and danced together, and sometimes three or four of them formed a set. That lively music was meant to dance to! Those tunes were often the highlight of the evening.

Years later, when I was newly married, my oldest brother was planning to go to a time in the hall. As we spoke about the upcoming dance, he began lamenting about how no one played the good old songs anymore, and how nice it would be to hear some of those songs. He said he'd love to, once again, hear tunes like 'The Jam on Gerry's Rock', but those old songs just aren't around anymore. Later that night, when I was almost asleep, I heard my husband ask, "What in the world was Wallace talking about? The Jam on Gerry's Rock?" Apparently, my husband had been thinking 'jam' was something you put on toast, and he knew my brother had a son named Jerry. He could not make sense of the song title, and dissonance disturbed his sleep. I explained to him that Wallace once worked in the woods logging with our father and grandfather. The jam was referring to a log jam, and Gerry's Rock must have been a place on the river. That song would have been something he could relate to and may have been meaningful for him.

That upcoming Christmas, I found an old songbook in the library with the music and lyrics to The Jam on Gerry's Rock. I copied it and wrapped it up like a scroll and tied it with a red bow with a dangling tag that read, To: Wallace From: Santa and left it at his door on Christmas Eve. I don't know if he ever got anyone to play it for him. Not having heard any more about it, I asked his wife, the following summer, if he found the scroll. She looked shocked and told me they found it that night when they returned home from their daughters. I had a sense that she may have been disappointed to learn that maybe Santa didn't leave it there after all. Other than that tune in which he overtly expressed pleasure, I would say his favorite may have been 'Me and

Bobby McGee.' It was played at every dance, sometimes at his request, and he never sat it out. The band didn't sing it like Janis Joplin but more like the Kris Kristofferson or Roger Miller versions. He loved it! It was wonderful to see him dancing and enjoying the music the way he did. He was a hardworking man and the music relaxed him, along with a little spirit perhaps. Recalling his love of music and dancing is a great memory.

The music brought the greatest pleasure. But not all pleasure was derived from the music alone at those Saturday night dances. I recall one Saturday evening dance that stood out because of a particular event I had only witnessed one time in my life. A sheer, outlandish surprise! During the band's intermission, some people had gone out to get fresh air away from the cigarette smoke that filled the hall due to people smoking indoors in those days. Some wanted to cool down their body heat generated from dancing. It was then I saw my niece sitting on a chair on the other side of the dance hall. I went over to say hello to her. I sat beside her and we chatted for a bit.

Soon the band reassembled. Just as they began playing a tune, we both noticed from the corners of our eyes someone standing before us. We both turned to look. There stood a tall, slim man whose brown, penetrating eyes were focused on my niece. He held his right hand out toward her and asked the one-word question, "Dance?" I turned to look at my niece just as her eyes dropped to the floor. This was not a moment of shyness on her part but rather the commencement of a body scan. I watched her eyes as they registered the cowboy boots and traveled up those long black pant legs, only hesitating a second to capture some of the details of the embossed belt buckle, before taking in the black vest looking casually draped over the plaid shirt with the lariat hanging down its front. Her eyes rose higher but did not stop at his moustache. They continued surveying the brim and top of the black cowboy hat with its silver-colored band. It was then they began their descent to gaze into his eyes and respond with her one-word reply, "No."

She turned back toward me, and he moved on; probably picking up his guns at the door. I had never seen anything like that whole encounter. I remember thinking; *I wish I had her brass.* I later wondered if it had been the plaid shirt that evoked her refusal. A black shirt may have made the difference as she could have imagined she was waltzing with Paladin.

My dad always had music playing in the house, and when he was there alone, it was his company. When I was very young and he would come home from work to spend his weekends with us, I couldn't wait to sit on his knee as he sat in the rocking chair to have a smoke. I remember one song he sang to me because I had just started school and the lyrics piqued my interest. The song connected us as my dad had also been young once and had gone to school. He sang a song called The Blackboard of My Heart recorded a year earlier by Hank Thompson (1956). Dad must have learned it from hearing it being played on the radio in his truck. He knew all the words!

As Dad aged, he was not like his son, Wallace, who longed for the 'old tunes'. In fact, when Dad was in his late eighties, he was getting a kick out of Garth Brooks. I don't know if it was the music or the lyrics he found so enjoyable, although the fiddle playing in those songs could reach out and grab you. Dad liked to recite poetry. His rendition of Brooks' songs was not so much to sing the lyrics, but more to state them with a big grin on his face. He enjoyed reciting lines from It's Midnight Cinderella (G. Brooks, 1995). His grin told me that he clearly knew where that slipper was. A couple of years later, he was smitten with the lines from Cowboy Cadillac (G. Brooks, 1997). His thoughts must have resonated with Garth's, that she looked good no matter what direction she was headed. Dad wasn't one to go to the dances, but at family celebrations, he'd get up to dance. I thought he couldn't dance worth a lick! I know. I tried dancing with him a couple of times. I don't know what those steps were, but the word 'jitterbug' comes to mind. It's really not for me to judge. He may have known perfectly well what he was doing, and thought I was a terrible dancer! Regardless, he loved the music and the lyrics. I wouldn't have changed a thing. It might have been less painful, but I'm so glad I danced with him. I wouldn't have wanted to miss out on dancing with my dad. I believe Garth would understand.

It was sometime in the late 1980s when I had a dream that was every bit as memorable as my dance hall experiences. In the dream, I was accompanied by someone I could not see. I sensed it was my spirit guide as I had often experienced the presence of this invisible companion in my dreams. I was taken to a small, rectangular, one-room building that was made almost entirely of glass. Everything inside was in shades of white. I could see through the glass, and the guide opened the door for me to walk inside. There were two steps and I climbed them to enter. (I later came to think this was a rather interesting detail.) Inside was an aisle with gurneys lined up on either side, totaling about eight or ten. Everything was pure white and on each gurney lay a skeleton. I was told that these are my ancestors. Suddenly the skeletons begin to quiver and rattle around on the gurneys. I'm not kidding. There was a whole lotta shakin' goin' on! I calmly asked the guide, "What are they trying to say?"

Then, the skeletons began to speak. They said they died with some regret of not bringing forth their music because the music was in their bones. "The music is in the bones!" I woke up. Even with decay, the music was still there in the bones. That dream is as vivid today as it was over thirty years ago when it occurred. It felt like they were telling me this must never happen again to anyone. It felt as if they were telling me that music is not just soulful, it is in our bones. I was so moved, yet saddened. I sensed that these ancestors had not sung or played or danced enough while they lived, bringing forth the music that was in them. The music that is in all of us! Music to be released for the full enjoyment of our lives and to be shared with one another. It seems essential for life to be fully lived. It was as though my ancestors wanted me to know this; like a message from scripture ensuring my joy in life would be complete. *I have spoken these things to you, that my joy may be in you, and your joy may be made full. (John 15:11; Online WEB Bible.)*

We have often heard of soul music, or that music is in our souls. The many great musicians from Motown connected us with soul music along with the wonderful jazz musicians who seemed to be able to bring their music into our bones. But from my dream, I had received a new message; that the music is more than soulful. It's more than that. The music is in our bones! The imagery in the dream was so powerful that it wouldn't leave me alone. It didn't feel like a funny dream, but one that was bringing me an important message. I spent time in reflection. Why was I being given such a message?

It was then I realized that music was not so much a part of my life anymore. I rarely had music playing at home as the television was always on. My husband and I had not gone dancing in a very long time. I didn't even know where people might still go dancing. It seemed that weddings and New Year's Eve were the only occasions left to express such joyfulness. Even New Year's Eve celebrations in recent years have become house parties with plenty of food and alcohol but no music or dancing. It may have been the excessive drinking, however, that led to the lowering of inhibitions resulting in the boisterous, off-key outbursts of Auld Lang Syne at midnight. At least that was something!

I realized the only music I had listened to in quite some time was in my car while driving. I knew the absence of music from my life had taken some of my joy away. It was time for a revision. I put music back into my life and even some occasional dancing; sometimes it was just my husband and I twirling around the kitchen floor!

By the time I had that dream, Elton John had already recorded Sad Songs (1984). What relevant lyrics! It reminds us that even in difficult times it is the songs and the music that we need. They do reach out and touch us gently, bringing release and restoring hope.

The music from the old world and from any ancient eras and all cultures, for that matter, is always with us for it remains in our bones and is passed on to us. Just as the vibrations of nature, the sounds of the birds, trees, waters, and all living creatures give rise to a rhythm and beat that can soothe us. Neil Diamond sang that a beautiful noise even rose from the street and the rhythms of city life. Musical sounds are not just alive in the hills; they're everywhere. We are the music. It is in us and in all life around us. Just listen!

Science even got curious in its efforts to understand music better. Throughout the past several decades, scientific research has shown that music is more than entertainment. Music is used as medicine to reduce pain, lower heart rate, muscle tension, and blood pressure; just to name a few of its health benefits. It alleviates symptoms of anxiety. Move over laughter! Music may now be the best medicine! In fact, it seems that ever since the beginning of time, music has had beneficial effects on humans, and it may be the reason music has been incorporated into many healing rituals throughout the world. Emotionally, it helps us deal with grief, sadness and anger. It is my understanding that scientific research has found that when we sing, the music and rhythmic vibrations resonate with our bodies and affect our electromagnetic fields. There are many studies suggesting rhythms can communicate bio-information that governs a variety of bodily functions.

My thoughts return to my siblings, our past, the love we shared for music, and the healing joy and laughter it brought to us. The only other musical interest I knew of in the family was that at my grandfather's house, there was an organ in the living room. I remember sitting there pumping on those pedals, I could barely reach, to make it sound. When I was eight years old, my grandfather died. I was there in his house afterward when someone uncovered a fiddle that had been packed away upstairs. None of the adults seemed to know why Grandfather had it or who it may have belonged to. I remember the moment and the sense of awe or wonderment that seemed to permeate everyone around me. It felt magical. Hesitantly, I reached out and touched the violin. I was told I shouldn't do that. I didn't feel bad because something in me told me I should. It seemed breathtaking. I have no idea what happened to the violin or the organ. I do know they were once in my grandfather's house.

I recall a couple of times, hearing older siblings make comments about how nasty or mean Grandad was to them. Each time I recall staring at them and thinking, *You must have been really bad to make* Grandad *mean*. I have only good memories of him. Sometimes I'd follow him into his house when he went inside to have a rest. When he was settled into his rocking chair beside the window, I'd climb on to his lap; sometimes even before he got his pipe lit. With one arm around me and one hand on his pipe, he would let my little fingers explore the deep wrinkles on his tanned and weathered face. Sometimes I'd hear him humming something inside him. He never told me to stop or to get down. We just rocked quietly together. Once he asked his housekeeper, who was fussing around the kitchen, if she had any cookies in the pantry. The pantry was just behind the rocking chair. She said she thought so. Granddad said, "Well, get her one." The housekeeper went behind the curtained doorway and returned with a sugar cookie for me. You see! There was nothing mean about Granddad. He carried a song inside him. Maybe those older kids just got out of step.

Many years later, as an adult, I stopped by my childhood home where my dad lived alone. As I walked into the family room, I caught an ordinary moment and a glimpse of my life in a flashback. There sat my father in his rocking chair, smoking his pipe and holding one of his little great-granddaughters on his knee. The flashback came and went in a second, but the love I felt in that room still lingers. After our greeting, Dad asked me if I would check that tin can on the counter and bring in a cookie for the little one. I smiled as I happily obliged.

It seems to me that just like cookies, some make music for themselves and some will share it with others. We participate in the shared music by singing along, connecting to the lyrics, and our bodies resonating with the vibrations and beating of the sounds. Those rhythms take us in their flow and make us want to move our bodies, enabling us to further share in the joy through dancing.

Recently I was at a dance where I was filled with joy just watching all those couples on the dance floor gyrating and moving their bodies to the upbeat classic the band was playing. One couple caught my eye and, having never overcome my childhood propensity to stare in disbelief at oddities, I watched them intently. It was a puzzle for me to try to solve. I tried to figure out what tune they were dancing to as not one movement in either of their bodies corresponded to the beat of the music with which everyone else seemed to be moving. My reaction to this observation was even shocking to me. I felt embarrassed for them. I wanted them to stop! Had they stripped off their clothes and stood there naked, I would have felt more comfortable and less embarrassed for them. My eyes flashed around the room to other observers and noted that they were also seeing this abomination. But they were only flashing glances at the couple and diverting their eyes to seem discreet. Not me!

I had to figure it out; there must be something I was missing. I also caught the looks of joy on the faces of these two dance partners. They looked like they hadn't been this happy for a long time. Finally, my resolution to this dilemma was that they were dancing to their own rhythm, their own beat; the vibrations in them that the music stirred. And between the two of them, there seemed to be some awkward kind of resonance. I figured the music wasn't creating a synchronicity with their own vibrations, but it was enough to stir theirs and bring forth their own joy. In my mind, I could only imagine how difficult it must be to move to a separate beat while another is being played. I thought it must be even harder to do than singing a descant in a song. Whether someone is singing a different line or a dancer is hearing a different beat, there must be some level of difficulty involved in staying focused. Eventually, I calmed down and accepted that they were happy dancing to their own beat. I was happy they were enjoying themselves.

While I find it difficult to understand, I can accept that not everyone loves music like I do. I love most genres of music. However, I don't relate well to Hip Hop/rap. It is not something I can dance to. My body does not resonate with those beats. My son told me there are powerful messages in rap music and I should listen more closely to it. His comment reminded me of a quote I once read that was attributed to Abe Lincoln. It was something like, 'I don't like that man. I must get to know him better'. I decided it was good advice to apply to rap music. I realized the lyrics often spoke of a world and culture I did not know so I could not really make connections or resonate with it. However, I believe that what we are to know will find its way to us and will resonate with us.

Recently I heard a song, 'I Can't Breathe' (Deitrick Haddon, 2020). This song didn't make me want to dance. In fact, it stopped me in my tracks. This is not soul music or some ditty we can tap our toes to or tap out on the steering wheel. This is music and lyrics for our bones and from his bones. Through our bones, with our bones, and in our bones! The music and lyrics may be the medium through which we can deeply reach one another so our suffering and needs are felt and grasped in the bones. Some music touches our souls or minds or hearts, but if those parts of us do not hear or do not allow the music to move us to care and compassion, to equality and respect, then we need the kind of music that allows us to grasp its message in our bones.

Our life on Earth begins with our first breath and ends with our last breath. If we can't breathe, then we have no life. Breath matters! If it is being taken from us by the brutality of others or by viruses we can, but don't contain, then, perhaps, we have to register this message more deeply; like in our bones! We need to care more deeply about one another and all lives. If music can reach our bones and communicate its message into our bones, perhaps it can change how we perceive one another, and change our behavior. Perhaps the energetic vibrations of the music incarnate in our bones and could guide us to not just think or give lip service to what is right but to act on what is right.

When Eminem popularized hip hop/rap in the late 1980s, it was clear the music was in his bones. With his song, Lose Yourself (2002), he sent the world an important message from his own realization. When the music is part of you, when it's in your bones, you can't ignore it without destroying a part of yourself. Music gives us the opportunity to be fully alive and to realize our potential. It seems to me that Eminem was wiser and made a better decision than my deceased ancestors had made.

Once when I was visiting my son on the West coast, I had a delightful experience. I was enjoying reading stories and singing songs to my two-and-a-half-year-old grandson, Andrew, and his eight-month-old sister, Lauren. Andrew had just crawled off my lap following a bedtime story when his mother brought to me Lauren's bottle of milk that she had taken at bedtime. Lauren came crawling toward me in the rocking chair, and I picked her up. She cradled into my left arm while she drank her milk and I sang, 'Twinkle, Twinkle Little Star', to her. When I finished the song, Lauren pulled the bottle from her mouth, bolted upright, looked at me, and did not take her eyes off mine as she hummed the entire tune back to me. It was a sight and sound to behold! Her parents, her brother, and I all stared at her, amazed. When she finished, she snuggled close again and continued drinking her milk. Not only did she get the tune, she memorized it immediately. Now, in her teens, her musical enjoyment seems to be in playing her ukulele and guitar.

In high school, my oldest son played tenor saxophone in the school band and traveled and played in Kiwanis festivals with the band. When he went away to university, he stopped playing except for when he was home at Christmas time. Then, he would accommodate my wish to hear him, once again, play a favorite of mine, Ode to Joy. It never gets old! My other two boys taught themselves to be very good guitar players. My middle son formed a band with some of his friends and together they shared their music with guests at various clubs and bars.

As I reflect on the love of music I've always known, I am reminded how much musical talent has been expressed by my grandparent's descendants. I believe this would please our ancestors. Four and five generations later, the music lives on and still shows up in the bones. Yet with some, it is still as hidden away as my grandfather's violin! Some have timid natures, but they do let the music speak through them, if ever so privately. Others have grown to share their musical talents with the larger community and the world. We are a big family and I don't know of all the musical proclivities of each one, but I do believe that loving the music, sharing it, and passing this treasure on to the next generations is like unlocking their genetic code to joy. It's already in their bones!

One of the most moving and tender moments I have ever witnessed on Facebook was a video clip posted by my nephew's daughter. It was her dad, son of my brother, Wallace. He was rocking his baby granddaughter while singing to her, the Yellow Rose of Texas. It was a witnessing of pure love as he gazed at her tiny features and sang to her.

It didn't stay on her page for long. He's bashful and probably told her to take it down. After all, it was a very precious and private moment he was sharing with his granddaughter. Yet, anyone who got to see it was surely blessed. It may have felt extra special to me because that nephew is the 'spittin' image of my grandfather; his great-grandfather. Yes, the beat does go on!

Some may believe they have no musical gift or talent, yet the joy they experience when others share their musical talents with them must surely be a reflection of their own musical projections. There is music hidden deep within them that is experienced in the pleasure and appreciation they have for the talents of others who express their music. We all have it in our bones, and if we would allow it, the music could ignite us and light up our lives to help make us whole and healthy people. Never hide that light or dim it in any way. Allow the music to be expressed as it wants to be. The Lord of the Dance in you still wants to dance. It's high time you joined in the dance.

Sharing the heartfelt gratitude of Abba, I too say, thank you for the music!

Jane Newcombe

Being raised with the foundation of a Christian faith in a caring and loving family, I experienced the teachings of Jesus as a way of life. I have grown to understand that these practices of 'a right way of living' are common to all the major faiths and religions. We were a large family and each one of us was welcomed with love, joy, and gratitude. Yet, not all children are received in this way.

The story is told in the gospels that Jesus took a child in his arms and announced to those gathered around that whoever receives a child in his name receives him, and the one who sent him. 'In his name' means belonging to him or on behalf of him. This statement, it sounds to me, is proclaiming that if we welcome a child with love (in God's name), we have also received Christ and the Father simultaneously in that child. It is part of the child's essence.

How will children know how much they have been blessed if we do not raise them with an awareness of the goodness within them? If children go astray, how will they find their way back to themselves, to their goodness and redemption? As Christians, we were told we were born in the image and likeness of God. There is no way any reasonable person can stand in front of a mirror and see a reflection of God, unless, of course, God looks like every one of us. Then, we might want to ask our reflection that same question Jesus posed about his identity, "But who do you say that I am?" Do you see the real me; the goodness within me?

At one time, no one concerned themselves with their ancestry unless they were royalty or had the occasional ancestor come back from the grave to haunt them. Of course, a ghost can't be killed, or hidden from. It is like your shadow. You must come to terms with it. If they search for you, it will be haunting. It may be the ghost of a once-wounded child who haunts us for having obscured the truth. Perhaps we haunt ourselves for that very reason.

Humans have lived through wars, plagues, and famines. They were grateful to have survived those sufferings and had a chance to live their lives and procreate. The dead were dead, and the living were trying to stay alive as long as they could. They weren't looking back through records to see who they were or where they came from. It seems to be the goal of ancestry searches to look back and wonder about our origins as if to try to place ourselves in our belonging. We belong to ourselves first and foremost with Christ and the Father included in ourselves. We are a creation and we must continue creating ourselves to our fullness. Our genealogy won't do that for us. Yet, searching for one's ancestry has become a fashionable diversion.

Some people are famously known only by their first name. However, the family name is important. Many individuals are recognized by the surname of the family they are born into, and the family name itself suggests to the community both heritage and character. In genealogies, it's the paternal line that usually identifies children and families.

Deviations from societal rules or secrets of community members were often known and sometimes hushed. Silence on such matters seemed to serve as a protection. But there have always been those in the community invoking the notion of sinfulness as a means to hold others down and make themselves look like they were somehow better. They may be the ones through whom truth can be revealed, although their reason may not be for truth's sake. Projection is always our struggle. It is the evil we must battle. This still continues.

When I told a family member I was writing a story titled 'Jane Newcombe', there was a burst of laughter followed by the remark, "I hope you haven't connected us to her!" My response was a smile of gratitude for having been gifted a good example of projection. My immediate task was to hold the reins on the therapist within who wanted to dig deeper and ask what it was about Jane that she didn't want to be associated with. It is the sort of question we can ask ourselves to enable us to get a look at our projected shadow because we all do this, some more often than others. Although neither of us had ever met or known this woman, at least one of us was willing to park something we don't admire in ourselves on her rather than consider it, examine it with our inner light, and take ownership of that aspect of ourselves. We all want to say, 'I'm not that'; but Truth says, I Am That I Am.

As people look behind them for their roots, they don't always have a family tree. Some just have tree stumps. If they dig those up, they may only find shallow roots, or root systems that are so entangled, gnarled in other roots, or broken that they can never expect to see a clear past there. Sometimes it seems that this 'dead-end' may be purposeful, and intended to keep us facing forward, looking in the direction we were meant to go. We can't go back. What does it matter where we came from? We are who we are, and who we continue to create ourselves to be. Should it matter if our ancestors were nobility or murderers? Will it make us sit up straight? Will it help us understand that 'urge to kill' we might feel when we are enraged by something? Shall we rest on our laurels or hide in shame? What outcome is expected? What is it in us that wants to stir the secrets and underpinnings of the past? Are there restless souls needing peace and urging us to uncover their hidden truth in historical searches? There are some people who simply refuse to look. Some look ahead. Others look back, but the wise and developing souls look within. Our hauntings may be our clue as to where to look. Might it be that our redemption lies beneath our inner darkness? Will we find the real treasure of who we are hidden there?

As I sat on the cushioned bench at the hall table writing out some thank you notes, I suddenly felt as though someone was seated beside me to my right. From the corner of my eye, I glanced and saw a very petite woman sitting next to me. I sensed she was very old, and she appeared to be dressed in earlier-period clothing. I turned my head slightly to get a better look at her, but she vanished. Perhaps, it was a breeze from my head movement, but before that, I had never seen a woman taken by the wind. I thought: How strange! I must be tired.

I continued writing my notes, but again, I felt her presence beside me. Without turning my head, I glanced toward her. I knew it wasn't my mother although she had passed away many years ago. I have felt her presence before, and this was not the same. I wondered about grandmothers. While my paternal grandmother was thin, she was much taller from the pictures I recalled seeing. My maternal grandmother was short like this woman, but not this petite as I recalled from pictures of her. Both my grandmothers were dead before I was born. I chose to think, based on height, that it might be my mother's mother. I decided to be polite and speak to her. I said, "Thanks for coming to see me. Who are you?" She didn't answer. But in my peripheral vision, I saw a bluish-gray dress with a wide collar and a lace trim on the edge. Her hands were folded on her lap in front of her. She seemed to be facing straight ahead. I again turned my head thinking I'd get a quick look at her face, but the second my head moved, she disappeared. I haven't seen her since, but I'm told she's around me.

Unable to see her face, I was reminded of the Old Testament story in Exodus, when Moses asked God to show his glory and was told, "I will cause all my goodness to pass in front of you, and I will proclaim my name, the Lord, in your presence, I'll have mercy on whom I will have mercy, and I'll have compassion on whom I'll have compassion. But you cannot see my face, for no one may see me and live." (Abridged from Exodus 33:18–23). I find it interesting for it is the face that holds the eyes, the windows to the soul. To look into God's eyes must be to look into eternity, to the alpha and omega, something that is unavailable to mortals. I am also reminded that it is the face and especially the eyes that newborns first seek for their focus.

An unusual experience like an apparition is not soon forgotten, but it is something one tries to put out of the mind if one can. As I lay in bed later, I thought more about this experience; wondering why such things happen. The first thing that came to mind was that she only appeared twice. I thought she could have shown up one more time. I'd always heard things happen in threes. Not this lady! Then I recalled that the number two is associated with 'witness' and 'support'. Thanks to the Pythagoreans and others who have attributed symbolism to numbers, I could not discount this. One, as it makes sense, is the number for singularity. She seemed to show up alone. I didn't see anyone else. But I thought, because I spoke to her, she knew I was aware of her presence and, therefore, I was a witness to her. Was she there to be a support to me in my aloneness, or was I to be a support to her?

In the weeks following this strange encounter, a number of synchronicities began to unfold. First, my friend invited me to go with her to see a psychic medium. We both wanted to 'connect' with loved ones who had recently passed. I did not know the psychic, and she did not know me. The first thing she asked was if I knew who the old woman was around me. I told her I didn't know. I was told this old woman was like a grandmother. She seemed Norse, and she wanted to tell me something. The medium passed on the message to me just as the grandmother figure had given it to her to say. At the time, perhaps in an egocentric state, I thought the message was for me or about me. It never occurred to me that it might be a message about her; perhaps something she thought I might understand or need to know. Recently, I have reconsidered the story's purpose.

Then, other oddities emerged. Conversations came up about family history, some directly and others indirectly but none of those conversations were initiated by me. Yet those talks did influence my thinking. I began wondering why there seemed to be such a convergence of this ancestry phenomenon over recent months.

One morning my son sent me a message and a picture of a young man who was searching for his mother. The young man knew his birthdate and birthplace as well as his mother's surname. It was also my son's surname. The message said the boy had been adopted as an infant and raised in a loving family. His sister was helping him look for his biological mother. My son wondered if I may have known who she was. I did not.

Later, while talking with my niece on the phone about spring cleaning, she mentioned that she had cleared out a cupboard at her mother's home that had a lot of genealogy books in it. I asked her if she knew the name of my grandfather's mother. I knew that my sister, her mom, had known it, but I could not recall it. My niece said she didn't remember, but she could look it up and let me know. Within a week, I had papers, books, e-mails, and messages concerning genealogies and historical information on family names. Only some of it came from my niece. Concurrently, my son sent me information on my family. It was researched by a man who had completed his father's (my husband's) family history. Without my awareness, this man researched my son's maternal ancestry. There was excitement in his voice as my son told me that my mother's family could be traced back to the early 1500s, and King Louis XIV was a relative. He added, "I knew we were f'n royalty!" However, on my father's side, he said the researcher couldn't get past my grandfather. I chuckled, thinking, nobody could get past my grandfather! What I did discover, among all these documents, was his mother's name: Jane Newcombe.

After many late nights and blurry eyes, I was able to trace my great-grandmother's family back a few generations. Although rarely inserted, there was information to indicate she gave birth to my grandfather. There is more intrigue and mystery as to who fathered him. While there is secrecy around that question, there was never any shortage of rumors. I began wondering if my visitor, the old woman seen around me, was Jane. After all, she is family, and I expect there is a purpose to her presence. Having a purpose is such a family trait!

The name 'Jane' is a Hebrew name meaning 'Yahweh is gracious and merciful'. Yet, 'Jane' is often accompanied by 'plain' or 'Doe', one expressing ordinary or nothing special, and the other implying unknown or unidentified. My Jane is neither 'plain' nor 'unknown'. She is my great-grandmother; my paternal grandfather's biological mother, the one who passed on her essence to him. In her essence, there was strength, determination, willpower, survival instincts, wisdom, awareness, and procreativity. We are bound together by our genetic codes, not by the time in history when we lived on earth, but by a mysterious coding and its dominance over time.

The name 'Newcombe', sometimes spelled without the last 'e,' simply means a newcomer to the area. But that is not how my great-grandmother was named. She was given her father's surname. She is the eleventh of twelve children born to Simon Newcombe and Frances Siteman on 20 June 1839. Her father arrived in Nova Scotia with his father and brothers; a total of six families of Newcombes from Connecticut, USA. Perhaps it was when their ancestors reached America that they were called 'newcomes'. I do not know where they came from in Europe or Scandinavia, but it may be that the surname was too hard to spell or speak so they were just called the newcomers. Changing a name makes tracing rather speculative. How many early immigrant names were simply called 'newcomer'? But a rose by any other name still has the DNA of a rose.

Even through blurred eyes, something was perfectly clear. In the genealogies, many families with different names had children they tried to hide. Children were referred to as 'issue', and some referenced as 'illegitimate', or 'father unknown', or 'believed to be fathered by'. Those babies were not conceived in vitro, they were legitimately conceived by natural means, the old-fashioned way. Probably, one hundred percent of the time, the mother knew who the father was. Yet, there were secrets. When will we ever learn that children are not something that can be hidden in the pantry with our cupcakes?

Secrets can hold both truth and lies. When a child is born, everyone knows by the evidence of a newborn that there is a newcomer to the family and community. The newborn has been received by someone in the name of love. But to hide its true identity is fooling and misrepresenting the innocent child. Hidden experiences and disguised facts seem intended to keep a seed of adult shame from sprouting.

But it will; for it gets planted in the child, and it will be an unwelcome surprise on the day it bursts forth. There will be no disguising the truth, for it is only the facts that have been made confusing and obscure. It is said that facts are based on data and truth is based on meaning. A person's identity is very meaningful! It says, "This is who I am." When a child is born, but given a false identity, is it truly welcome for who it is? A mortal being embodying Christ and the One who sent him? Is that not a child's birthright along with knowing its parents?

One day when the child finds out the truth and the facts, it will ask why he or she was deceived; and the answer will be, "I didn't want to hurt you." Generally, that reply compounds the confusion and does not lessen the pain. Truth (The Christ, the I Am the Truth, and the Life) is part of our identity, our very self. Not one of us will ever know our true 'Self' if we think someone else can face our shadow or examine our darkness for us. They cannot. Will Truth accept a scapegoat? We have to do our own repentance for our redemption. Secrets and a lack of understanding can project our shadow onto our descendants so that they, too, will not know who they are.

There are many people who will live and die not knowing themselves. I suppose there is really nothing unusual about that. Most of us won't do the hard work of withdrawing our projections, facing and accepting our darkness, and changing our ways to grow into more unified individuals. Many people who do not know their parentage may one day learn of it from friends, family, church records, or genealogies. The truth will come as a painful surprise.

In my great-grandmother's time, the children who were born to single women were often given away or merged into the woman's family and raised as siblings. Rarely was a child kept by its mother to be raised by her alone. While silence doesn't seem to be regarded as a sin (i.e., a wrong done to ourselves or others), its effects make it seem like a criminal act because of all that has been stolen from the innocent.

I imagine there was a lot of pressure and influence on the young woman, who was unwed, to get rid of or hide the child, so as to be unencumbered by her situation. Maybe being able to keep her child and have it raised as her sibling might have been the best option she could hope for. Maybe she secretly planned to tell her child the truth one day. Then again, maybe a long-kept secret seemed safe, and it shouldn't be disturbed. Until one day someone else tells the secret. That will be the moment when trust, belief, love, hope, and truth are all crushed. That may seem like the child's most vulnerable and darkest hour. The shocking truth will strike at one's identity; at one's personhood. Is there a more disturbing breach of trust?

How does one face all the family and suddenly realize not one relationship is what you thought it was? The child will wonder how far-reaching is this deception. Does the community know? My clergy? My teachers? My friends? Did everyone take part in the secret of hiding my identity? How can anyone be trusted? Why do people make truth or facts so difficult, so unacceptable? Why is it necessary to perpetuate lies? Why is so much fear generated around truth-telling, when it is lies that will torture the innocent, and return to haunt the guilty? The fear-based, short-sighted idea that truth might be bad for you might bring some short-term benefits, but it will definitely bring long-term harm. It is always the truth that is beneficial in the long run. It is always the truth that we are required to seek and follow.

It is not blended families or any family combination that is problematic for people. It is the deceit, denial, and the family members not knowing who they are in relation to one another that raise unnecessary problems. It seems to be right and a decent thing for parents to help and support their daughter and grandchild in their time of need, but creating dishonesty about the relationships is more than perplexing. It seems fortunate to me that every child enters this world as the Christ child bringing with it its own new light and all the potential for its own redemption.

I find it hard to imagine that a woman who bears a child would not, in some way, always think of it as hers. Perhaps it is possible for a surrogate mother to do that; I don't know. At least they know initially they have made the decision to carry another's baby. Yet, it seems there is something about renting that earliest connection between a woman and the child she carries for nine months that may leave a longing in each of them. Many women have given children up for adoption for a myriad of reasons, and those children were received, loved, and raised well. I expect there are some children who know they are adopted and have no interest in knowing their ancestry. The family who raised them and cared for them is their family and they don't need more. They feel blessed and are not tormented by their biology. But the biological parents may live with the pain of not knowing and wondering. I have never met a woman who does not quietly remember the child's birthday and whisper her love to and for that child wherever it may be. Fathers are not exempt from this pain either. When a man sees a child he knows is his, but must pretend he does not know the child because of circumstances that would not allow truth or relationship to develop, he is expected to remain silent. What good comes from this for anybody? What is generative about deception? Do these secrets not eat away at the soul?

Ancient philosophers have said the point of being here is to 'know thyself, and to thine own self, be true'. If they were right, it seems like it is a big hurdle and a blatant waste of time spending one's life figuring out one's ancestry. It seems an unnecessary diversion from our personal growth, withdrawing projections, and making peace with ourselves. Or is it? Maybe that is just some of the suffering we are meant to encounter on our way to redemption.

I don't know of the childhood/youth of my great-grandmother, Jane. Her birth was recorded, but it was not until the first Canadian Census in 1871 that I next heard of her. By then, she was thirty-two years old and living with her brother. Prior to that, her whereabouts seemed undocumented. Most of her siblings were married and had families. Like most unwed women of her time, she worked as a servant in the households of those who needed help and had the means to hire help. My grandfather and his children grew up without ever knowing her although she lived nearby. My father was nineteen the year that his grandmother, Jane, died. The only things we ever heard about her were tales and rumors surrounding her pregnancy for my grandfather. The stories that got passed on sounded like she was a young, loose woman running about with men.

There was a tale that the man who raised my grandfather was not his father, but just a good man in the community who was helping out poor Jane who wouldn't be able to raise the child on her own.

Strangely, how it was overlooked that Jane was already raising her daughter on her own. It was rumored that there was a guy, never spoken of with ill-repute by anyone, but with the inference of having a questionable character. The man was named, and I traced his genealogy. He was not a Kokopelli but was presented as fertile and joyfully intriguing. When the genealogies landed on my table, I began working on that puzzle.

In the Census information, Jane was living with her brother George, his wife (formerly, a young widow), and their children in 1871. In 1875, at the age of thirty-five, Jane delivered her first child, a daughter, Celestia Newcombe. This little girl was loved and raised by Jane. There is one mention of who is believed to have fathered her. Jane's brother George and his wife had a child born the same year. There is no exact record of how long Jane remained living with her brother, but she was not in his household in the 1881 Census. There was a tale that she was living and working in the household of George Hawes and his wife Sarah Hurd. If so, it would have been between the years 1875 and 1881. George and Sarah had nine children. One son had died as an infant and eight children were living at home, in the Hawes household, according to the 1871 Census, as was Sarah Hurd's mother.

Five years after her daughter's birth in May 1880, Jane, just four weeks before turning forty-one, had a son whom she named Walter Tyler, 'believed to be' Walter Tyler

Hawes. In the 1881 Census, the child is reported as living in the Hawes household and is named Walter Hawes. In one record, it is stated 'adopted'. (Adoption often meant that a child is left with a family so as not to be seen as 'illegitimate'.) Now there is a word I'd put in a gobbledygook dictionary. Legitimate means to conform to the law or rules. How can a child, born of its mother and conforming to the Law of Nature, not be legitimate?)

'Illegitimate' can only apply to some man-made rule requiring a mother to be married to the child's father. In the Census that same year, 1881, Jane Newcombe is recorded as living with her daughter and working as a servant in the household of George and Margaret Leslie. Jane later lived with her sister Johanna. The 1901 Census reported that Jane's daughter and son-in-law and their little girl, Vona, were living with her. In 1902, the son-in-law died at sea when the child was three years old. It appears that Jane, her daughter, and her granddaughter continued to live together.

The same name as claimed by the Kokopelli guy showed up six times in the genealogy records from the area. Five were eliminated as not possible fathers of Walter as they were either dead at the time in question or had not been born yet. Only one remained that could be a possibility.

He was a young man married with two daughters. At the time of my grandfather's conception, when Jane was forty, this possible stud was only twenty-four. Let's just say I wouldn't fault my great-grannie for that! This Kokopelli and his wife also had a son born the same year as my grandfather. Those intent on spreading this tale said that the Kokopelli stud later married and he and his wife had a son. This creation story makes their son the half-brother of my grandfather. In fact, there is no indication that there was another marriage for him, but he and his wife did have a third child, a son, born the same year as my grandfather. Even though the tale was told long after Jane's death, and even after my grandfather's death, by people born three generations later, it was told emphatically. Some of my family was told we are definitely from the Kokopelli line, and we are not Hawes.

I'm quite certain there are only two people who know for sure, and they are both dead. In connecting the marriage lines and the various relationships, it could be guessed as to who or why some folks would pass on, with such certainty, a story that may have been surmised to protect a grandfather and/or to berate Jane. Whatever its purpose, a descendant continued the tale for those who would believe it.

There may have been some need to protect George Hawes and the integrity of his family name from an adultery accusation. In some form of logic, it seemed reasonable to say that George was a good man, and he only took in his housekeeper's baby to raise because he was helping her. I think he would have been a good man to take his own son and raise him if that was an agreement he and Jane made. None of us have any idea what he told his wife. There was an unusual notation about her in the genealogy saying she 'could not read or write'. She may have had to mark her 'X' to adopt a newborn for some reason: fact or pretence. Some may have thought she didn't really know what she was doing. If George was the father and admitted it, he would not need to adopt his child. The record showing that Jane was no longer a servant in that household a year after her son's birth although he remained there, may mean that

George's wife no longer needed or wanted Jane's help with the chores. I am grateful to both George and Sarah for having lovingly received and raised my granddad. I am also thankful to Jane for giving him life.

George may very well have been a good man and one of passion and character. But he was not perfect. He and Jane were also not stoned to death which is considerable evolutionary progress. While Jane was not betrothed to anyone, both George and the Kokopelli guy were married men. In Luke's Gospel story, the woman who was found guilty of adultery was taken before Jesus. He knew it was a set up when they asked him what should be done with her. Roman law was enacted in the region, but under Jewish Law, it was required she be stoned to death. Jesus' reply to them exemplified the need to face our own shadows and withdraw our own projections. By telling them that the one who was without sin should cast the first stone. He was, in effect, directing them to first look within themselves and see their own sins and shadows because the first responsibility is to ourselves and to mend our own ways. The accusers turned and went home. The woman in the gospel is not condemned but is told not to do that again. That was settled. Maybe George and Jane had a look within, too.

This example from Jesus' teaching differs from the condemnation and punishment that was part of the old covenant and Jewish Law, but it is very similar to the fundamentals of Buddhism which believes that unwholesome actions (sins) emerge from our ignorance and can bring about our undoing. It follows that punishment and condemnation are not what's needed. Such individuals need instruction and guidance that will help to enlighten them and their future choices by showing them a better way. This is the wisdom that Jesus offers. We will experience the results of our actions.

I recall the message the psychic medium delivered to me that day from the old grandmother figure around me. She repeated to me the story of two people who were in love and could not be together. They were separated. He searched everywhere for her and endured loneliness, heartaches, and struggles. He climbed over a wall and escaped guards who were chasing him with swords. He landed in the garden where he found his long-lost love alone. As they embraced, he said to her, "I would have kissed the blades of their swords had I known they were driving me to you." Apparently, he was grateful for all the fear and suffering he had to endure for it had been through those experiences by which he found the way to the love he was seeking all along.

This nexus of ancestry, deception, and faith may remind us to take responsibility for discovering, knowing, and speaking the truth of who we are, and why we believe the things we believe. We must consider our own identity. Who do you say that you are? What could it mean to be received as one embodying Christ and the One who sent Him? This is what Christmas means to me. The celebration of every child that ever was, is, or will be because every child brings light, hope, and redemption to their world.

What We Believe Is True

As we sat at her table to enjoy lunch together, I felt it was time to share with Edie something I'd been hesitant about for a long time. I guess it was because I always valued our friendship. I knew she saw me as a kind, strong, and wise person in much the same way as I saw her. We are both women who have been through hardships and loss but always remain forgiving and devoted to our families and friends. I did not want her to think any less of me. I had kept this from her for a long time. I began with, "There is something I've been meaning to ask you."

Edie looked at me with questioning eyes as I blurted out, "Do you remember Ronnie Laws from high school?"

She answered, "Of course, I do."

"Do you think we look alike? Because quite a few people have said to me that he and I look a lot alike. They'd even ask if we were related, but we're not!"

I glanced at Edie who was studying me and when our eyes met she said, "You do look a lot alike. I always thought that too. There is a strong resemblance."

I continued before my fear could restrain me. "Well," I said as casually as I could, "one Friday night a bunch of us were walking home from the movies. Ronnie walked me up my street to my door and kissed me goodnight. Just a little peck. The other kids waited for him on the main street, but his brother had been watching us. I didn't know this until quite a while later, and Ronnie never did ask me out. Then one day he came up to me at school and said he wanted to talk to me. He told me that his brother Jack said we couldn't date because I was his half-sister. Apparently, his dad and my mom had an affair."

The silence seemed to last forever. Then Edie said, "Did you ever ask your mom about it?"

"Not right at the time. It was a few years later, but I did ask her, and she told me it wasn't true. But she did say that before she met Dad, she had a relationship with Ronnie's uncle, his dad's brother. Soooo, I don't know!"

Edie and I were looking directly into each other's eyes, both searching, and she saw that I did know. She also knew that I would not voice any betrayal of my mother.

When we are in that moment of facing a hard truth, the presence of quiet understanding is all we want. Edie also knew that the hurt I was hiding was not about my parentage. It was about the missed opportunity for my mother and I to share a private, personal truth that concerned us both. It was a death-like loss for neither of us could ever resurrect that topic.

The thing about my friendship with Edie is that we can be serious and thoughtful, or completely foolish and laugh hysterically over some matter that needs to be lightened up. We briefly changed the subject to our hunger and how delicious lunch tasted before I jokingly added, "You know I had a crush on Ronnie in high school. It's a good thing nothing ever came of that!" We both laughed before Edie began her speculation.

She said, "Maybe he had a crush on you too, and his dad found out about it. Maybe he let Jack know about it so he would tell Ronnie."

I answered, "I don't know. But I do believe my father is my real father because he is the one who took care of me and loved me. He was always there for me and took care of all my needs. I just can't think of that other man as my father. I don't believe that other man is my father!" It seemed forceful and convincing, but then I added more. "Although he used to be around the house a lot when I was really little. I think he was just a real good friend of my mother, but," I added with a burst of laughter, "I did call him daddy! Come to think of it, there was another man who often used to come to the house from down the East Section. I called him daddy, too. Maybe I just called every man Daddy!" I smirked as I noticed my plate was still quite full while Edie had eaten most of her lunch.

It was then Edie asked me, "What if, somehow, you got undeniable proof that the other man is your father; how do you think you'd feel?"

I replied, "Oh, I'm sure I'd feel very hurt. Yet it really doesn't matter. I can't change any of that. I am who I am!" But I thought, my dad is my dad!

Quietly, I reflected that I don't know about my ancestor's experiences or even what others may know, believe, or say about them, or about who I am for that matter. What I do know is who has cared for me and loved me, who has duped or mistreated me, and who has brought me hardships. I'll still choose to be forgiving, kind, and welcoming, but also discerning. I know who I am because I know who I have chosen to be. I could hear my phone ringing, jolting me out of my thoughts. By the time I left the table and located my phone in my purse, I had missed the caller, who was 'No Caller ID'. A message had been left though. Feeling somewhat frustrated, I sounded off with, "This is the third time he has called me with no caller ID and he never leaves his phone number in his message! How does he expect me to call him back?"

Edie asked, "Who is it?"

I said, "Oh, just Ronnie. I think he wants me to go to the Laws family reunion this summer."

Edie asked, "Are you usually in touch with him? Does he know you're sick? Is that why he's calling?"

Too many questions at once. "No!" I clarified. "I've just been hearing from him and his brother Jack a lot lately. I don't know if he knows I'm sick. Do you know Jack?"

"No," Edie answered. "Is Jack a younger brother?"

"Yes. And he and Ronnie came by the house a couple of weeks ago to see me. Jack said he was going for DNA testing and wanted me to do it. I told them I already did that swab thing and I have my ancestry information." I had to laugh then and told Edie that I'm not sure if the relatives I have in there are even my relatives!

At Edie's puzzled look, I explained. "Some people tell me that my father—the man I believe is my father—was actually fathered by another man, not my grandfather! Oh God! Some days I think I'm my own grandpa!" The two of us burst into laughter.

As we settled in for some coffee and dessert, Edie asked, out of curiosity, why these brothers were doubling down all of a sudden on trying to prove I was their sister. "It seems unusual," she said.

"I know Jack said to me just before they left the house that if it turned out that I was their sister, he would be very proud to call me his sister. I thanked him very much, but it didn't really matter to me. Now they are talking about me coming to their family reunion this summer. They have one every five years."

Edie wondered aloud if the boys had made some promise to their father that they were trying to carry out, and said it sounded like they were on a mission. She questioned, "What's driving them? Could it be a need to know the truth?"

I hunched my shoulders as we cleared the lunch dishes and moved to the living room sofa.

Suddenly Edie asked me why I went to live with my grandmother and aunt, and how old I was when I went there. She knew that was where I was living all through high school, but I guess we never talked about it.

I told her I was about five years old and I was going to be starting school. My parents traveled a lot because of Dad's work and they could take my brother with them because he was younger, but I was ready to start school. So, I stayed there and lived with them right up until I left home. I explained, "I used to go and stay with Mom and Dad sometimes though. I had my own bedroom there and they just lived up the road."

As memories flooded back, I laughed and asked, "Edie, did I ever tell you that I wanted to push Grammie down the stairs? Oooh; more than once I thought of it. She hated me! But she loved my brother! Whenever he came by for a visit,

I had to wait on him; go get him ice cream or something to eat. Oh, he was special to her. She just made me scrub the floors and steps, keep the house clean, hang the clothes out, and do the dishes… You know one time she fell down and she wasn't breathing. My aunt said she was dead and called the doctor. For some reason though she thought we had to pick Grammie up and put her into bed. So we hauled her up off the floor and rolled her onto the bed. And she started breathing again! All I could think was, oh shit. Isn't that awful?"

"I was such a horrible person! Another time she fell at the bottom of the steps and we had to get her upstairs and back into her bed. That wasn't easy! Grammie had dementia and we had to kind of fence her room off so she wouldn't get up and wander around and fall."

Edie suggested that maybe Grammie knew that Dad wasn't my biological father, so she may not have cared so much about me if I wasn't her blood. Grammie would have known who fathered my dad. Maybe because of that she accepted my brother more and thought of him more lovingly.

I said, "Well, she certainly treated him better. That's all I know. I still wanted to shove her down the stairs, and I always felt like I was a bad person when I had those thoughts about her."

Edie offered, "Anybody would have felt that way. You're not a bad person. In fact, you're a good person for not actually pushing her!" We giggled with the youthfulness of old friends.

When Edie went to the washroom, I reminisced about my children. My husband is the father of each one of them. There is no question about their parentage. Yet my daughter had children with different men, and she was not well enough to raise them. So, my husband and I, their grandparents, raised them because they are our blood. They belong to our family. But they each know who fathered them. I don't think either one of them ever wanted to shove me down the stairs though. I wondered if it was just me and my dad who didn't know our biological fathers; the ones who hadn't been told the truth.

I remember a little cousin, and playmate telling me once that I was not really a Bennett, but that I was a Fuller because my dad was really a Fuller. That evening I told Dad what she said. Dad was enraged and told me never to say that again. I had never seen him so angry. I wonder why he just didn't think that was a silly thing for my cousin to say. Why did he have to get so angry? Although I never repeated those words again, that same story was told to me several times through the years; sometimes with old photographs to prove resemblances. I had to admit that Dad, Mr. Fuller, and his son all looked alike. It seemed to me that everyone had his or her story, and they were sticking to it.

Now I wonder what any of those relationships meant if he was not my biological father. None of those cousins or any of Dad's people would be related to me. When Edie reappeared, I told her I had to get going as the afternoon was getting late. At the door, we hugged and said we loved each other.

On the drive home, I wondered if I'd ever live long enough to meet all those who wish to claim me as a member of their family. I would have an entirely new set of relatives. When Edie asked me, I told her I had not yet heard back on the ancestry testing. I couldn't bring myself to tell her that the results were confirmed. The Laws could rightfully claim me.

Only six months ago, I was diagnosed with cancer, and have been battling that disease so I can continue to live the life I already have. Now it seems like there may be another family and all new relatives waiting to welcome me. How strange life is!

Perhaps the love and bond that Dad and I shared was deeper than anyone could realize. Even if our blood or biological forces did not connect us, our bond was cemented by devotion, caring, and our belief in each other. I believed he was my daddy, and he believed I was his little girl. That's enough! Because what we believe is true. I now realize that Dad and I had something in common not shared by the other family members. We both had mothers who had affairs, conceived us, and kept the identity of our biological fathers from us. Yet, we had each other.

Now as I lay here on this hospital bed, I face another unwelcome truth. The hope I clung to for a recovery, or at least more time, was futile. There is no hope left. My friends and family who are gathered in this hospital room with me are some of the many people who have loved me. I fade in and out of their conversations. Edie comes to my bedside, kisses my forehead, and tells me she loves me. I manage to open my eyes, take her in, and tell her, "I love you, too." It takes all the energy I have, but it is how we always say goodbye to each other. I know I will soon make my departure. I also know my brothers, with whom I've never had a sibling relationship, will come to my funeral to say goodbye because they too love me. We are all truth seekers. I now know that both this and that are true when it comes down to who we are and who we love.

The Boys Who Played Ball

The stands and all the grounds around the field were filling up. It was twelve-thirty. Gametime wouldn't be for another two hours. Yet, it was no surprise as Friday's paper carried a notice that the stands would fill fast for the deciding game in these finals. It was expected that one of the largest crowds ever assembled on the Eastern Shore would be at the Billy Bollong Memorial Ball Park on Saturday to witness the Maritime Intermediate 'A' softball championship game. Were the Spry Harbour Atoms ready for this day? Probably, they had a great ball season! First, they made it to the Provincial semi-finals that went the limit, defeating some strong teams along the way. After beating out Brookside in the quarter-finals, they went on to defeat the Berwick Legionnaires in the semis to become the mainland champs.

Such wins come about, not just because a team has a strong, solid roster but because those players have their hearts in the game. They loved the sport! Guys like Mike Boutilier, the Atoms' youngest player at only seventeen, was one such example. He was an usher at his friend's wedding on 1 September 1962 when the first game against Berwick was scheduled. Thankfully, it was one of those Catholic, morning weddings. Following and maybe during the ceremony, Mike was thinking about the game, and his uncle offered to drive him from Sheet Harbour to Berwick if he wanted to play.

In the game of softball, as in life, you've got to seize opportunities when they arise. Mike approached the groom and said, "You don't need me here anymore, do you?" He was released; removed that dapper attire and got into his ball uniform to make the two-and-a-half-hour drive to the game. He made it in time for the start of the fourth inning. The coach, Hanson Josey, came out of the game and Mike went in. It was a good decision. The Atoms won the opener that afternoon in the thirteenth inning. Mike's double brought home Wade Josey to break the 4-4 deadlock and score the winning run. The following day the Berwick team traveled to Spry Harbour where the Atoms won their second straight game, with Wade Josey, again, scoring the winning run on Ernie Dougie's single in the last of the ninth for a 2-1 win.

The Atoms had claimed victory in the semi-finals on the mainland and would go on to play the semi-final champs from Cape Breton, the Point Edward Cubs, to earn the right to represent Nova Scotia for the Maritime trophy. These two teams were strong contenders. Game one of the best of three was scheduled for Cape Breton. The starting pitcher for the home squad was the same guy the Atoms had trouble hitting the year before, in 1961.

That year, the Atoms had traveled to Cape Breton to play the Westmount team for the Nova Scotia championship. They lost out to that ball club and did not advance to the Maritime playoffs. Nineteen sixty-one was the first year the team played with ball gloves. It took the players some time to get comfortable with that contraption as they had always caught balls with their bare hands. It was in that same, close game that fielder, John Fahie, dropped a fly ball and was so upset with himself, he threw his glove away! Not all was lost though.

These final games always concluded with a celebration and an after-party which can also serve as a calming salve on the wounds of defeat. The libation and laughter are shared by all even when the umpire takes a walk outside into the backyard of the house party, and falls down a newly dug well. Snorky, as he was affectionately named, was a respected and well-loved umpire. He stopped by the house, at the coach's request, to help the boys celebrate. He was a good sport. The story goes that he was wet, but alright.

Nineteen sixty-two brought in a new year and a renewed hope. The Atoms had earned another chance to play for the Provincial championship, and they were determined to drink from the cup of victory at their own celebration party. The starting pitcher for the Cubs could throw an elusive ball. His pitches came in fast, and he made it look like they were perfect strikes coming across home plate. But they weren't. Those pitches were lifting and curving to the outside. They were balls, not strikes. Coach Josey was on the sidelines yelling to his batters, "Make him come to you! Make him come to you!" The batters followed his instruction and, rather than striking out, they began walking to first base. That only lasted a couple of innings when the Cubs' coach pulled his pitcher in favor of a new arm. Not wanting to leave the mound, the pitcher appeared to be more than disappointed. But that's the way the game's played. It wasn't until the seventh inning that the 2-2 deadlock was broken with a three-run homer by Mike Boutilier. The Cubs never fully recovered. The game ended in a 7-6 win for the Atoms. Ernie Dugie was the winning pitcher in game one of the best of three in the 1962 Provincial finals against the Cubs.

The following weekend, the Atoms were defeated on their home field by the Cubs who walked away with an 8-3 win. In the third and deciding game that followed, the Atoms had a 12-6 victory. Not only were their players strong defensively, but they were also hitting the ball like their lives depended on it. Third Baseman, Wendell Hawes had a triple, double, and single, just a home run short of the cycle; Carmen Josey, Short Stop; Richie Owen, Catcher; Carmen DeWolfe, Second Base; Mike Boutilier, Centerfield; and Pitcher, Jack Ferguson all had a pair of hits in that game. They made winning look easy! That weekend, the Atoms captured the Nova Scotia Intermediate 'A' Softball Championship. They were now eligible to play the New Brunswick Champs, Newcastle Creek Grand Lakers, who had already taken victory over the champs from Prince Edward Island.

The Atoms were a team of skillful players with excellent coaching and, in 1962, they were stronger and more confident than ever. They had already won twenty-six out of twenty-nine games in Intermediate 'A', and had won twenty consecutive games during the season within their own Eastern Shore League. Having captured the Provincials for the year, they were only two wins away from taking the Maritime Championship.

The next weekend, the Atoms would travel to Newcastle, New Brunswick, where the teams would meet at five o'clock on Saturday, on the Newcastle field. The game went an extra inning with Newcastle plating the deciding run in the bottom of the tenth for a 5-4 win. This meant the final showdown would take place in Spry Harbour on Saturday, 6 October, Thanksgiving weekend with Newcastle taking on the hometown Atoms. The Atoms would have to win both ends of a double-header to prevent Newcastle from walking away with the prized trophy. If there were to be a second game, it would be played one-half hour after the end of the two-thirty game.

An outdoor stage/platform had been erected near the field a couple of weeks earlier. It was quickly designed and constructed to hold the band and dancers who came to celebrate their team's Provincial victory on that weekend. On Thanksgiving weekend, all the fans would be there again, hopefully, to celebrate the Atoms' Maritime Championship victory; or, worst case scenario, to concede defeat and celebrate Newcastle's victory. Only Newcastle wanted that outcome!

Along with that structure, the excitement had been building in Spry Harbour and among the Atoms' fans for the past few weeks. Plenty of extra hotdogs, soft drinks, and other favorites were ordered to meet the expected demand at the concession stand; a 6' × 8' framework was attached to the back of the neighbors' free-standing garage that bordered the ball field. No one called it a 'concession stand' in those days. It was called 'the canteen'. Even though the property and owners changed hands, the canteen continued and grew to become the General Store in the community.

Owners Connie and Sherman Hawes would cater to the grocery needs of the area for the next thirty years adhering to the economic principle of supply and demand. During the ball season, however, Sherman was often the umpire. He was covering home plate for some of the early games back in the fifties, stationed behind the catcher, wearing only a face mask for protection. In the sixties, he would go on to earn his Nova Scotia Provincial Umpire accreditation and wear the official protective equipment. He continued to serve as umpire for many official ball games. His childhood polio had limited his participation in the competitive play of softball, but it did not hinder his keen eye for calling the pitches and plays.

It seemed everyone had made preparations for the championship game, and you could feel the excitement in the air. The press would be there covering the plays and taking photographs of the champs following the win. The Billy Bollong Memorial Ball Park sign even looked fresh in its bright blue and gold colors matching the jerseys and jackets of the Atoms ball club.

Billy Bollong was one of the boys who played ball with all the friends of his youth in the late forties and early fifties. Many of his friends would be playing in the championship game. Back then, those kids didn't have a real ball field or uniforms. For the love of the game and outdoor fun, they'd gather on Maple Hill in Spry Bay. Some referred to it as a cow pasture, others, as a rocky farm field. To these youngsters, with their balls and bats and a few who had gloves, it was the ballfield. If these boys were to be found in the summer, that's where you'd find them; on Maple Hill. The young ones, just old enough to be there, were included with the older boys. Billy was one of those older boys.

After graduation, Billy chose a career in the Air Force. He left home to go for his training and was later posted in Goose Bay, Labrador. In 1956, at the age of twenty-three, Billy was killed in a vehicle accident at the base. His family and friends at home mourned his loss. Some of those boys he'd always played ball with wanted to organize a competitive ball team. The Josey brothers, Hanson and Densmore, with their vision and determination, were instrumental in getting a team of community boys together to play competitive ball. But if they were going to play in more advanced leagues, they needed a new ball field. In those days, Spry Harbour was a close-knit community, and there were lots of large families and young people experiencing their lives together and caring for one another. It was Billy's dad, Leo Bollong, who donated the land for the ball field on which the Josey brothers' dream would be realized. It was the parcel of land they would one day call their home field. It was named in Billy's honor and became the Home of the Spry Harbour Atoms.

A labor of love ensued converting the land to a ballfield. The adults in the community as well as surrounding communities supported these young men in their quest. It was arranged to have a surveyor from the pulp and paper mill in Sheet Harbour come and survey the property. Then someone from the area, who had a dozer, came and did the initial work of preparing the foundation for the field. Much of the rest of the preparation was done by locals and the players themselves; carrying wheelbarrow after wheelbarrow loads of rocks, and raking and raking and raking until it looked like a ball field. A back stop, dugouts, and benches were then erected.

Billy's brother, Glenn, said that when they held the official opening of the ballpark on Sunday afternoon, 11 June 1961, a big crowd was gathered. There was an unveiling of a monument dedicating the ball field to the memory of LAC Billy Bollong of the RCAF. The newly formed Spry Harbour Atoms Athletic Club presented a plaque to Billy's parents, Eileen and Leo Bollong. It was first blessed by the Parish Priest in the area. The first pitch was thrown across the plate, ceremoniously, by the local Councilor, Arthur MacKenzie with Leo Bollong at bat. Before tossing the ball in, Councilor MacKenzie asked, "Are you ready, Leo?"

Glenn said, "Dad had a swipe at it." He added, "There was a loud round of applause."

Soon after the ceremony concluded, the Atoms hosted a double-header with Chezzetcook Aces, another team in the Eastern Shore League. The Atoms won both games, the first with a score of 13-11 and the second game 14-3. Densmore Josey was relieved by Ernie Dugie in the sixth inning of the first match. Pitcher John Fahie went all the way to take the Atoms to their win in the second game. In a later game that season, when no home run had yet been hit over the fence at centerfield, it was heard and told among the players that Leo Bollong said he would give five dollars to the first one who hit a home run over the centerfield fence. It was about the fifth inning and the bases were loaded. Wendell Hawes was at bat. On the first pitch, Wendell swung, hitting the ball over the centerfield fence. It was gone, and you could tell that ball goodbye! There was a lot of excitement. As the players rounded the bases to come home, other team members and a few fans were at home plate to give Wendell a handshake. Wendell recalls Leo being among them. He said, "When Leo shook my hand, I felt something and looked down. He had put a five-dollar bill in my hand when he shook it." Wendell smiled and raised his eyebrows.

He continued saying, "That was something! That was like a half a day's pay!"

There were no 'Go Fund Me' or team sponsors in those days. Every cent was raised through the initiative, ingenuity, and hard work of the team Coach Hanson Josey, Captain Densmore Josey, and Manager Orrin Hawes with the support and cooperation of their team members, family, friends, and community. Everything from a few cents on bottle returns to profits earned from card games of forty-fives or cribbage, dances, picnics, community suppers, and selling tickets for prizes donated by local retailers helped the boys gather the money they needed for jerseys, caps, balls, bats, bases and other necessities to play the game. Sometimes the players had to contribute a few dollars themselves toward the cost of their uniforms, but mostly their funding came from the organization and leadership of their coach. With his vision, determination, commitment, and awareness that these boys were good ball players, Hanson was motivated to take his team and join the Eastern Shore League in 1960.

The Atoms weren't looking back; they were looking ahead. In 1961, they won the League trophy and got to play for the Provincial title that year. They didn't claim it. But the following year, they would take the Provincial championship and go on to play for the prized trophy, the Intermediate 'A' Maritime Softball Championship. That was an exciting day, not to be forgotten by anyone who was there.

As the newspaper reported, an exceptionally large crowd did gather. At two o'clock, the cars were lining the sides of the main road; not another one could get near the ball field. Fans had already filled the bleachers and were sitting on top of the dugouts and hoods of vehicles that offered them a view of the field. There were lineups at the canteen, and the players were warming up. When the two umpires arrived, the game was about to get underway. Double-header games were seven innings rather than the usual nine.

In the second game of the Maritime finals and the opener of Saturday's twin bill, John Fahie pitched the Atoms to their 6-2 victory forcing a third and deciding game.

Jack Ferguson toed the rubber for the Atoms in the final. Newcastle came to Spry Harbour intending to take home a trophy. They started the deciding game with a determination to win. They struck fast with a run in the first inning. Ferguson, and the team, kept Newcastle at bay until the sixth inning. By that time, the Atoms had a 4-1 lead. Mike Boutilier had hit a two-run homer, Garnet Josey a solo, and Wade Josey had made it around the bases to home plate. In the sixth inning, Newcastle got three hits; the damaging one, a three-run homer, knotted the score at 4-4. Coach Josey couldn't let that continue. Ernie Dugie took over in the seventh inning. Densmore Josey led off the bottom of the seventh with a single. Ernie Dugie was next at the plate and hit a fly ball that was dropped in the outfield. Densmore didn't waste any time rounding the bases and crossing the plate. It was that run that broke the tie and gave the Atoms their 5-4 victory and the Maritime Intermediate 'A' Softball Championship proving their prowess as some of the best softball players in the Maritimes. On that day they were, indeed, proclaimed the best softball team in the Maritimes!

It was the Atoms' victory that would be celebrated with music and dancing! However, it wouldn't be until September 2018 that the Spry Harbour Atoms, 1962 Maritime Champions, would be inducted into the Maritime Sports Hall of Fame in Halifax, Nova Scotia in recognition of their achievement.

But the 1962 ball season wasn't over for the Atoms. The following weekend, in mid-October, the Atoms would play the Westphal Withers team at Spry Harbour in the deciding game for the Eastern Shore Softball League (ESSL) crown. The League winners would also receive the Halifax Herald Trophy. The Atoms were easily victorious, walking away with a 14-3 win. The ESSL President presented the trophies to Captain Densmore Josey and Coach Hanson Josey. Densmore pitched the win, giving up eight hits which brought Westphal their three runs. The team made two field errors. Hitting home runs were Garnet Josey and Elwood Owen.

In 1962, the Atoms played a total of 33 games, including league games, semi-finals, and finals for Provincial and Maritime trophies. They won 30 of 33 games. There was talk and some consideration of moving to the Senior 'B' League. But that was not the choice. At the time the competition level and strength of Senior 'A' seemed a better fit for the Atoms, and they were welcomed into that league. In 1963, the Atoms became the eighth team to join the Senior 'A' Softball League in Halifax-Dartmouth.

But before moving on, one must take time for reminiscing and reflecting. Prior to Senior 'A', Intermediate 'A', and even before the Eastern Shore Softball League, exciting competitive ball was being played by the Spry Harbour Atoms. Originally, the Atoms played in what was known as a Sheet Harbour loop league in the 1950s. They joined the Halifax County Rural Softball League at its inception in 1957. Back then, Mike Boutilier was the batboy for the team.

One summer, a young man studying to be an Anglican minister came to the area. He wasn't going to fit in if he didn't play ball, so he often found himself on Maple Hill. The story is told that he could hit a ball. One day he did just that. He drove the ball beyond the field perimeter and into the woods. The unfortunate thing was that of the two balls the boys had, this was the last one they had to play with. The game had to stop until all the players went into the woods to find the ball.

Nearly all of the local boys played ball on Maple Hill. Some said that every boy in the community played ball even for a portion of a season. Many of those kids were spotted wearing Atoms' jerseys in a game. Several moved on from playing their sport, but all remained big fans of their team. The team signed new players. Some of them came to the Atoms because they still wanted to play ball after their own local community teams had dispersed. Some wanted to be in a league that was planning to play more competitive ball with teams outside their area. Lloyd DeWolfe, Carman

DeWolfe, John Fahie, Richie Owen, Ernie Dugie, and Elwood Owen all became team members of the Spry Harbour Atoms by 1960.

By 1961, batboy Mike Boutilier was old enough to play on the team and covered centerfield. He handed over his former job on the team to Gerald Josey. Mike was young and fast and excited to be playing on the team. In an early season game, with Ernie Dugie on first base, Mike hit a long drive. As he ran round the bases and past second, he also passed Ernie who was on his way to third base. Mike had to go back to second because Ernie wasn't going to make it past third. He only did that once.

The Atoms won the Halifax County Rural League crown in 1957, the first year the league existed. In 1960, the Atoms again won the Halifax County Rural Softball competition for the second time in four years. They had a great season in 1960 and, for the Rural League title, defeated a robust Spryfield team 3-1 in the best-of-5 final. The first two games were played in Spry Harbour and by the time the dust settled, the series was tied. Next up was a double-header the following week on the Halifax Commons. Whoever won the first game would be one victory away from becoming the champs.

John Fahie pitched the Atoms to a 20-13 win in the first game. He also clubbed a seventh-inning homer among his three hits. Richie Owen also starred in the game with four hits. These new Atoms were demonstrating what assets they were to the team and would continue to prove they belonged with the local boys and their caliber of playing ball.

Just before capturing the Halifax County Rural Softball League championship, the Atoms had won the Eastern

Shore League pennant and playoffs with series wins over Chezzetcook Rovers and Westphal Admiral Taxi. In 1960, the Atoms' Eastern Shore League and playoff record was 28 wins and 7 losses. In two more years, they would take the Maritime Championship in Intermediate 'A', and 1963 would see the club move on to the Senior 'A' League.

This cohesive team of young men, who had consistently played ball together for over five years while playing in more than one league at a time, had honed their skills together and had an awareness of one another on the field. They played the game like a fine-tuned instrument. Their respect and appreciation of one another, along with their good sportsmanship, whether they were victors or losers, won the team the admiration of all.

In the games before Senior 'A', there were bruises and scrapes and, definitely, calloused hands in the early days, but there was rarely if ever, an injury in a game that was so severe to put a player out of a game and, certainly, never out for the season. This was not the nature of the game when it was played well. An incident that stood out because it was unusual occurred during an exhibition game in Spry Harbour against the Brookfield Elks. Carman Josey, trying to score a run, slid into home plate and his cleat spiked the catcher. In what was likely an automatic reaction to the surprising pain, the catcher took a swipe at Carman, who responded in turn. As the scuffle began, a zealous fan and friend of Carman ran onto the field to fight with the catcher. This was promptly responded to by a fan and former Atoms teammate. He was a big, strong man. He hurried onto the field, picked up the zealous fan, and carried him out of there. Everyone had a chuckle as play resumed. No one was injured.

Things would be different in the Senior 'A' league. Unbeknownst to these boys who played ball, they were entering the beginning of the end of ball playing as they knew it.

In 1963, when the Atoms entered the Senior 'A' league, they were playing against seven other teams: O'Malleys, Halifax Olands, Stadacona, Shearwater, General Bakeries, Kline Motors, and Dartmouth. During their first three years of Senior 'A,' the team was still called Spry Harbour Atoms and retained many of the local boys who had played ball together. In this new league, the Atoms continued to play ball as they knew how. They had fun. Early in the season, Mike Boutilier, who was a fast runner and a track and field star, hit a double. The next batter, Wendell Hawes, hit a long drive to the centerfield fence. As Wendell ran along the third base line to home plate, he was only a few steps behind Mike. A fan yelled to Wendell from the sidelines, "Are you the guy who's the track star?"

Wendell answered, "No. He is," as he pointed to Mike. To this day, he's not sure how he caught him. He guessed that Mike must have just slowed down. They scored two runs.

Early in the '63 season, Wendall Hawes led the league with a .471 batting average with 17 officials at-bats. Ernie Dugie had spent more than a half dozen years developing his untouchable skill in whip pitching. In the first six games played in the season, Dugie was considered 'the king of the league'. The Atoms won three of those six games and the wins were attributed to Ernie's pitching. There was some aggression in the ball games played that summer. In June, Ernie Dugie was sidelined by a leg injury received while fielding a ground ball. There were also injuries received by other players in the league. The Atoms continued to play effective ball.

In early September, it was Richie Owen's home run in the ninth inning of the last season game that helped take the Atoms to the finals. It was his second home run of the season, but in that same game, he also hit a base-clearing triple. Jack Ferguson had been pitching when Ernie Dugie, playing the outfield, was called to the mound. The Atoms held a strong lead of 11-2, but now it was the bottom of the ninth and O'Malley's had brought in their sixth run of the inning, had the bases loaded and no outs. Finally, the Atoms made their first out on a ball hit in the infield. Then the key play and second out came when Richie Owen reached far over the rope barrier to the right side of the backstop and caught a pop foul from O'Malley's batter. With two outs and the bases loaded, another batter was at the plate with the opportunity to bring in the tying or winning run for O'Malley's. Instead he bounced the ball back to Dugie who jumped for joy and ran to first base making the final, and unassisted, out himself. During the game, Ernie Dugie contributed three hits while driving in two runs for the Atoms. In that game, Ernie Dugie and Richie Owen were quite a team!

In an earlier season game against O'Malley's, an excellent ball player and star of that team, was running home while the ball was being thrown in from the outfield. Richie Owen was reaching forward to catch the ball. O'Malley's runner jumped over Richie's head to avoid him and to land on home plate attempting to score the run. While he was still airborne, Richie turned and tagged him before his feet hit the plate. Now; just close your eyes and imagine the cheerful roaring of the fans on that play, and you might come close to hearing it. It was loud!

Richie Owen was not only a solid batter, he caught just about every ball thrown at him for many years. Whether it was the pitches of his teammates, Densmore Josey, John Fahie, Jack Ferguson, or Ernie Dugie; reaching to make the out by catching those seemingly out-of-reach foul balls; or covering the plate to catch the fielded ball being thrown toward him so he could tag out the runner coming home, Richie made the play. Knowing where the play needed to be made and executing it efficiently was one of his skills. He could pick up the bunt, and drive it to Wendell Hawes to get the runner coming to third base out, knowing that Wendell, 'the gunner,' could put that ball in the mitt of the First Baseman in time to get the batter out. That was the excitement and skill level these guys brought to the game. It was said that once when Hanson Josey was playing first base, with his foot on the bag and his glove held up as a target, he heard the first base umpire yell, "You're Out!"

He's reported to have said, "It all happened so fast, I didn't even know the ball was in my glove!" Wendell's accuracy and speed, just like Richie's catching skills and decision-making, could be relied upon by their teammates and fans. It is understandable that Hanson may not have realized the ball was in his glove; although it was a sound the umpire would have been listening for. Hanson had been accustomed to catching the ball in the outfield with his bare hands. In fact, he caught a fly ball once with one bare hand before gloves joined the game.

The June 1964 roster had eleven of the Atoms players remaining on the team: John Fahie, Carman Josey, Ernie Dugie, Wade Josey, Densmore Josey, Richie Owen, Carman DeWolfe, Michael Boutilier, Wendell Hawes, Jack Ferguson and Coach, Hanson Josey. The other four Atoms' players came from other Senior 'A' teams. The team was still called the Spry Harbour Atoms. When the Senior 'A' league selected their All-Star Team that year, Ernie Dugie and Wendell Hawes were the only players selected from the Atoms' team.

By 1965, some of the Atoms players had decided to play softball in the new Marine Drive League which was a replacement to the Eastern Shore Softball League. Additional teams had been added to this new Intermediate 'D' League which included a Spry Harbour Atoms team. Work and family commitments contributed to the players' decisions. It was good that they made the decision when they did for later the players would need official permission from the league to drop down a league after being in a Senior league, and only three players would be given permission to do so. After entering Senior A, some players recognized sooner than others that something was different. The game had changed. There seemed to be very little 'sport' left in it. They wanted to get back to playing the game they knew. Yet, in some way, they felt committed, like they belonged to the Spry Harbour Atoms. That's who they were.

By 1966, there was no longer a Spry Harbour Atoms team in Senior 'A'. Sponsorships and league finances resulted in team name changes and players moving around. The Atoms had become Olands Atoms. In that year, Olands Atoms were playing Greenwood. Wendell Hawes was playing second base. He was running backwards to catch a fly ball that he had called. It was his. His new teammate, from Olands, came running in from centerfield to catch the ball. He crashed into Wendell. He knocked himself out and knocked Wendell down breaking his nose and fracturing his jaw. As Wendell lay there on the field, he heard someone yell, "Where's the ball?" He just raised his left arm and opened his glove. There it was! He could be centerfield! Wendell was out for some of the regular season games recovering from surgeries He later would play in a Senior 'B' league as would Mike Boutilier. Wendell went on to play for other teams and coached several teams. He also coached an Intermediate 'D' team for a season. He loved the sport.

The following year, 1967, Ernie Dugie was pitching for the Halifax Keith's team, and in 1968 helped them win the Senior 'A' Provincial title. Mike Boutilier also played for Keith's in 1967. Some of the boys who, for years, had played ball together as a team were now playing against each other. Wendell Hawes and Carman Josey were playing for Dartmouth Mooseheads, and Carman DeWolfe played for an Eastern Passage club for a season. By 1967, only five of the original Atoms' players remained in the Senior 'A' league.

Softball, as the Atoms had always played it, was a changed game at the Senior 'A' level. It was a more aggressive game resulting in more serious injuries. Several players were physically knocked out. Once their sport and fun time, the game was becoming a risk to maintaining their jobs and supporting their families. Some players even termed the game 'grudge ball' or 'win at any cost' ball. These boys had known sportsmanship which was no longer evident to them in the game.

By 1970, many of the Spry Harbour Atoms were still playing ball, but not in the Senior 'A' league. They wanted to play the game as the sport they had known it to be. Most of those players returned to play ball for another ten years or so in the Marine Drive League where they would again play on the Spry Harbour Atoms team; this time in Intermediate 'D' Softball. They were once again playing their sport against local teams like Ecum Secum Eagles, Sheet Harbour Rockets, Chezzetcook Aces, Tangier Tartans, Jeddore Sharks, and teams from the Ship Harbour area.

It was there that the fun of the game lived on for the boys who really knew how to play ball. The boys, who played ball with sportsmanship, respect, and for the love and excitement of the game, were once again the Spry Harbour Atoms. While interviewing some of the players still with us, it was profoundly noticeable how those 'long-ago boys' still feel admiration and respect for one another, and the skills each one brought to the team and the game. Each one of them expressed, "What a great bunch of guys we had on the team!"

Can you hear it? The resounding 'Yes' from your fans! We will always remember that some boys playing ball and having fun brought such joy to their fans and such purpose to the community. Their integrity, sportsmanship, dedication, and desire to be their personal best while they played a game they loved, for the fun of it, resulted in much more than tangible trophies. These boys set an example of what real champions do.

Keeping Vigil

It was Easter morning and I sat in the pew of the rural church with my husband and three sons, ages nine, twelve, and fourteen. The church would have been full for the Easter Vigil, but there were only a few families, maybe thirty or forty people along with a partial choir for the morning Mass. Although I wanted to attend the Vigil and knew my vote was weighted and influential, the boys and their dad voted to attend the morning Mass instead. I was aware of their humorous knowledge, 'When Mama ain't happy, ain't nobody happy', so I knew they would be willing to concede if I insisted. I wanted to keep them happy, so I agreed to morning Mass. It was something I would regret.

Apart from the Easter lilies and hydrangea that decorated the altar, it seemed like a usual Sunday Mass. After the priest, whom I will call Father Wayward, finished reading Matthew's gospel concerning the risen Christ, he began his homily. Then he stopped and said, "First of all, I'd like to see a show of hands of all of you people here who really believe that Jesus rose from the dead." He insisted, with a mocking smirk on his face, "Anybody who really believes that Jesus rose from the dead and went up to heaven, put your hand way up so I can see." My head felt as congested as an early morning traffic jam with thoughts cramming in from everywhere. This was not an opportunity for discussion of our beliefs or of our reflections and understanding of them. Besides, this guy, this representative of the person of Christ, was smirking!

Every Sunday, as a family and with our community of believers, we said the Creed at Mass professing 'this' is what we believe. In solidarity with what my children had been taught by me and my religion, I raised my hand as I stared at the priest. I noticed my husband and sons then raising their hands; probably in solidarity with me. The priest did not wipe that grin off his face. I turned to look toward the other side of the church and behind me. I saw only two others in the congregation with their hands raised. I did not see the choir. I felt frozen. I heard Father Wayward say, "You can put your hands down now," but it felt like we'd already been robbed. There was some unsupressed snickering from some of the 'audience' as if they were in on some kind of joke with the priest. I don't recall his homily although it seemed like I was listening for some kind of connection he would make between our faith and the risen Christ. If he made one, it was lost on me. The Mass continued with the pall of pretense that filled the church and laid my faith to rest.

From my childhood, I had learned to try to find the good in everything. It is there if we just look for it. This experience was instrumental in provoking a discussion within our family about our beliefs, and how we experienced and understood our faith. Unfortunately, during that same time, Holy Week of March 1989, news had just broken about the scandal within the church and the Mount Cashel investigation in Newfoundland. This had stirred real concerns for many. My boys had heard these news reports. My sons were not altar boys but some of their friends were. Those were issues the two older boys raised in our discussions. The early teen years are sensitive and confusing enough for developing young men. Having to question their faith and the stability of their beliefs and trust along with the other, more typical, changes of teen life was influential in the trajectory of their lives and faith. Fortunately, their values, our family values, were ingrained as a way of life and would not be shaken by something outside of them. They had a solid measurement against which they could evaluate right from wrong.

The years passed and the two younger boys chose to not be confirmed or married within the church. They detected a hypocrisy that was uncomfortable and didn't fit them well. I have watched and am aware of how my sons have chosen to live their lives by following a strong value system that encourages kindness, generosity of spirit, and respect for others. They do not suffer fools gladly but show patience to a point. They know their own self-worth and are able to honor it.

More than thirty years have passed since that Easter morning. I have spent those years struggling with my own faith and beliefs. I recalled my son, in his late teens, asking me out of his own bewilderment, "Mom, how can you, of all people, follow a religion that has been so disrespectful to women? The Catholic Church has gone out of its way for hundreds of years to persecute women, and yet you keep defending it!" I heard him but I didn't really listen to him as he continued on his diatribe citing times and events of the abuse of women by the Catholic Church. My seemingly duplicitous values were confusing to him. He woke me up to a deeper examination of what I hold true and valuable.

Today is Holy Saturday and, just as in Rome hours earlier, darkness has fallen. With the wonder of technology, I can join the Easter Vigil from the Vatican as if in real-time. Perhaps, I mean earthly time, for time itself is quite an illusion but we seem to have harnessed it, based on the rising and setting of the sun. I have arranged my candles in preparation for the Vigil and will participate as much as I can, here alone, during this pandemic.

Following the Old Testament readings where we are reminded of God/Yahweh's deliverance of his people from bondage, the Vigil moved to lighting the Paschal candle and passing on the light to one another. I light my candles and imagine my source to be the same. There are no baptisms due to Covid, but we do renew our own baptismal promises. We recall our symbolic purification with water and anointing with oil. We're told the Light was brought into the world, not with the sun's appearance but, with the birth of the Christ child.

In John's gospel, the 'Word made flesh' refers to Jesus, the Christ. I realize that John's gospel intends for us to understand that Jesus, and only Jesus, is God in human form. Might this be one of the first turns of the screw? Surely, from the beginning, the Word of God or divine energy resided in all of creation. This New Testament construct was to denote their God had made a new covenant with them, and that the Old Testament promise would be fulfilled through a new Christian mythology.

Easter is the Rite of Christian deliverance and salvation. The Christ child, the Light that came into the world at Christmas, is now Christ the Redeemer. It is the time of year we celebrate our deliverance from darkness. Christ is attributed with saying, *I Am the Way, the Truth, and the Life…* It is only by following the divine that we can find our way back to our beginning and our essence, That Light is in us and never completely diminished in anyone. It is always with us. As long as we have breath, we will have the light of the divine to show us the way to truth. The truth is what will set us free and allow us to bring about a new life for ourselves.

During my life, I have attended Mass in several different languages and have always been able to follow along. Language makes no difference to the meaning or the message during the Eucharistic part of the Mass. The ritual and symbolism transcend words. The soul understands and participates in the uplifting transformation that is more divine than music or a smile. At this Easter Vigil and to my surprise, Pope Francis read from the Gospel of Mark. I could not recall Mark's gospel ever being read at an Easter Vigil. It was usually one of the other three gospels, most often Matthew's.

In Mark's gospel, the women who have come with spices to anoint Jesus' body are told, by the young man sitting inside the tomb, that He is Risen and to tell the disciples to go to Galilee for he has gone there ahead of them and they should follow him there. (Think about that. He is risen but he is gone to Galilee ahead of them. What does it mean to be risen?) The Pope emphasized that God always goes before us, and despite all of our failures, it is always possible for us to begin anew.

If God is present in all creation, or in all people, then we can imagine God was present in all those who have gone before us. We are not the first nor will we be the last to experience suffering. Suffering isn't new; God has known it before we did. How? Probably because God was present in all those who have gone before us and have suffered. It is not that the particular circumstances or situations evoking our pain are the same, but the resonance and vibrations of the various degrees and depths of human suffering have been known and experienced by others and the God within them. They were not alone in their suffering and we aren't either.

It seemed significant to me that the Pope pointed out how obtuse the disciples were. He said they were always with Jesus, but very often did not understand him. Pope Francis focused his homily on what it meant to return to Galilee. He said it meant: to begin anew and return to the place of the first encounter; to set out on a new path as shown by walking away from the tomb and grief and; to allow ourselves to be surprised by God. He added that it meant to go to the periphery, and to the most vulnerable for no one is least and no one is excluded. In our defeats, God opens new paths and hope is reborn. What a beautiful, truthful message!

It seems to me we are all born with our own God-given light, and we can have that light dispel our darkness anytime, even when we are most vulnerable. It allows us to have a good look at ourselves and return to the truth. We are not least or excluded. But we can choose to be. We can and often do choose to be less or excluded by what we falsely tell ourselves about being unworthy instead of holding true to the divine that says we are worthy and loved. You are God's creation, and if you do not see that Light in those around you, whatever you do, do not turn away from your own Light. It may be the only one amidst the darkness. All that is asked of us is to surrender to our suffering servant role.

It is both personal and collective. We are in service to the divine, which is our higher self. In order to fulfill that role and have the fullness of life, we must endure the pain and suffering of withdrawing our projections, those thoughts and beliefs we cast onto others, ourselves, and the universe. We must release and turn away from our desire to cast those stones. We must choose a better way for ourselves, and be an example of a better way for others. It is through and with and in the divine that we find the truth, the way, and subsequently, the life. This is not some religious concept. This is a sacred everyday presence. Religion is a thief that has tried to hijack this presence and this notion from us, and has tried to convince us the only way divinity is available to us is through religion. We have been brainwashed to link divinity to religion and churches, and just as some behaviors of churches and religions repel us, some now treat divinity as an accomplice. Divinity is part of us and our world. It is not owned by religion. It is yours and mine. It is that which is our higher, better self.

A friend of mine told me that she noticed that I nod or bow my head and smile when I meet or encounter people. She added that in her Eastern culture greeting or bowing of the head means 'the divine in me recognizes the divine in you'. At the time, I wasn't consciously aware of doing that, but I am now. I am also now aware that I get the same response from others. Often when I'm walking and pass by someone, there is a brief glance and nod of our heads. Sometimes people will not make any eye contact, and they look the other way. It's as if they choose not to acknowledge the divine in you, and they do not want it acknowledged in them. Perhaps, they are on their way to church, and never realize they missed the encounter.

There was an expectation about the messiah and his coming to save the people and lead the Jewish nation, and Jesus didn't look or act like the one expected. It seemed like it would take some convincing. If the people were to believe Jesus was a God, as they understood Gods to be, He could not be less than the mythical Gods who had miraculous births and rose from the dead. Rising from the dead would be a requirement for the Christian God. Paul says in I Corinthians, if Christ is not risen then our preaching is useless and so is your faith. So, you better believe it! It makes me wonder if Father Wayward thought his preaching and our faith were useless.

The ascension is a great expectation; yet, for all humans to modify their behaviors in the way Christ taught us must be a greater expectation because very few seem to be doing it. Why is it easier to believe in a Risen Jesus who will, at the end of time, take us to join him; than it is to believe that we can experience an inner transformation, have renewed hope and a new life, enabling us to really show respect and care for one another here and now? When Jesus said, "Love one another as I have loved you," I think he meant now, not later. Jesus already taught and showed us how to live that love for one another now, in the present moment.

Recently, I was reminded of how we were discouraged from reading the Bible as young Catholics; primarily because we would not be able to understand and interpret it ourselves so it would only confuse us. We were to rely upon and trust in what we were told and not question it. Being part of the flock meant you did not question the shepherding even if you wondered that you might actually be corralled by a big, bad wolf. The motto seemed to be: No need to think, just believe what you are told! In the event of irregularities, you seemed unable to reconcile, you were advised to pray for stronger faith so as not to stray. In other words, double down on your trust with what you've been told, and ignore the wisdom or enlightenment that emerges within you. Learn to not trust yourself!

I shiver at the thought of the collective implications of such guidance. Without independent or critical thinking and self-trust to carry us forward, would we not all be stagnant and enslaved? It would surely take a miraculous parting of our deepest emotions to release us from such bondage. As I recall, disobedience was the original sin, and it seems to me the church has been disobedient to Jesus' teachings and has held the faithful hostage to church laws rather than prioritizing and teaching, by example, the timeless messages for humanity that Jesus taught. Perhaps, in this 'cancel culture', it is Truth that has been canceled.

An awareness of the presence of Christ with us every moment as our Way, Truth, and Life is attainable. It's God in us. It knows what mischief we're up to anyway; no sense pretending it's not in the room or part of our energy. I think if we try to be aware, our experience will be as Pope Francis said, God will surprise us! Our own resurrection will be no less amazing than the crocuses and daffodils that emerge from the dark, dank, and damp soil of early Spring; that time of renewal, resurrection, and rebirth. We, too, can be redeemed and reborn; or in plain language, we can change for the better. We can become better people. Why just look at those lilies in the field and any of the other miracles around us! How can the resurrection and life not be within us too?

Although Communion was not administered at the Vigil due to Covid-19, the Eucharist was celebrated. I heard myself say, "Lord, I am not worthy to receive you…" I suddenly wondered why we say that. Is it a pretence of humility or an outright defiance? In my belief, God loves us and never abandons us. We are never alone in our darkest places. God is always there with us. Just as those who require their God to be physically and literally risen from the dead, I would require my God to be ever present with me, not gallivanting around somewhere else. How could we, and why would we, imagine a God who does not find us worthy? I have heard that He created everything, and found that it was good!

I've never heard any exception to that story, like, perhaps, those humans who were created in His image and likeness were not really so good or worthy. Maybe, every day, we could just say, "Thank you for finding me worthy." Maybe, if we stopped resisting. Maybe, if we stop telling ourselves we are not worthy, we might stop behaving in unworthy ways and make better choices for ourselves. When we say those things, it is only ourselves we convince of our unworthiness, for God knows better. If God or Love has shown us we are worthy, who are we to say we are not? I am reminded of a young mother who was laughing and telling me that as she stood waiting at their front door for her six-year-old son, she watched him as he stopped in front of the hall mirror, looked at himself, and proclaimed, "You are loved." From out of the mouths of babes! Perhaps we could all start our days with such an honest reminder as we glance at our reflection and at the image and likeness of our God who wants us to know every day that we are loved.

When I was a child preparing for my First Communion, the second question in my catechism book was, 'Where is God?' The answer I was given to memorize was, 'God is everywhere.' My older sister who was helping me and my brother with our instruction showed some annoyance with me for my inquisitiveness. I was stumped by this response that God was everywhere, and my seven-year-old mind wanted clarity. I asked, "Is He in that chair over there?" as I pointed across the room. "Is He sitting right here beside me?" And as I held up my hand, extending my little finger, I asked, "Is He in my little pinky finger?" Each time, my sister kindly and patiently answered, "Yes He is."

But by the time I got to my 'pinky,' I saw the kindness fading from her face, and I knew she wouldn't take this line of questioning much longer. I stopped questioning God's whereabouts, but I never stopped thinking or wondering about it. It was never on my radar that somewhere in the world nonlocality and quantum entanglement were being proposed or researched. Perhaps it would have informed me that God could be everywhere at the same time. However, I do remember the day it dawned on me that if God is everywhere then God must exist as energy. Since then, I have thought of God as the energy of love and creation. I know that love and creation are in everybody!

There are those who aspire to be associated with position, power, and affluence. They judge such people as more worthy and will give their respect and reverence to them. A God or a human with a humble and simple nature or lifestyle, whether suffering or not, is not as attractive to some people as Gods or humans who have powerful, dominant, and opulent attributes assigned to them.

An example of this preference comes to mind from a fishing trip I was on a few years ago. I was invited to go salmon fishing with a friend on the pristine Bonaventure River in Quebec. While salmon fishing is restricted to catch and release and the use of barbless artificial flies, for their protection from extinction, there still remains the business entrapments, employment, and lodging that was established to encourage the holiday and relaxation experience of the well-to-do-sport fisher. My friend and her husband had bought a timeshare for seasonal fishing, and he had forfeited his time to allow me to go there as his wife's guest. They would normally share a cottage, but I was treated to my own.

After a beautiful day on the river, we were having dinner with the only other guests there at the time. We dined at the main lodge in the dining room after having drinks and appetizers in the parlor. The other guests were two men, Michel and Jean, who had traveled from Montreal. Together we sat around a common, elegantly set table with candlelight and wine enjoying the four-course dinner served to us. After chatting about our day on the river and who had seen or rolled a fish, my friend, Jeannette, asked the men if their wives ever went fishing with them. Michel, a gentleman whose demeanor was humble and thoughtful, always tried to speak to us in English although his first language was French. He answered Jeannette's question with a shake of his head and a facial expression I understood to mean that fishing was not something that would interest his wife.

Contrastingly, Jean asked my friend if she was foolish. He said, "We don't tell our wives we are coming to a place like this! My wife thinks we are somewhere in the woods in a shabby old camp eating wieners we roasted on an outdoor campfire while we are being eaten by bugs. She doesn't want to go there! So, I let her think that."

We all laughed. Then, Michel asked about our summer plans and if we'd be doing other fishing trips. Jeannette, nodding toward me, said, "She's going to Italy the day after she gets back to Halifax." She then spoke directly to me saying, "You really should go to the Vatican while you are there. It was the most wonderful experience of my whole life being at the Vatican and seeing the Pope!"

Michel nodded and said, "Yes, my wife and I went last year and saw Pope Francis."

Jean interjected with, "I've met him, but I've also met the real Pope."

Michel looked at his friend astonished and questioned, "The real Pope?"

Jean looked back at Michel and replied, "Yes. Jean Paul II. He was a real Pope! This new guy; I've met him but he just wants to live in a small house and drive around in a little car." He then made a sour face and shook his upper body in disgust. All eyes were lowered as if to hide their respect for humility. All eyes except mine. There is a difference between wondering and knowing if something is true.

As I watched Jean, I knew that he had never enjoyed a Big Mac in his life; so I asked him, "Where did you meet him, at McDonald's?" That moment sprung the needed release of tension as my friend burst into laughter, and Michel had to set his wine glass down on the table as his hand and body were quivering with his attempt to control his laughter. I diverted my eyes from Jean after I saw the blush of embarrassment flush his face. The server came by and the conversation shifted.

It was at university that I studied the Old and New Testaments.

Years later, as a catechism teacher, I had a refresher course on the New Testament taught by a priest who had recently returned from the Holy Lands. Mark's gospel, believed to be the earliest written, about 70 CE (both the sun and the Christ denote earthly time) claims to have an anonymous author. If that's true, it may be a way to infer a question of credibility, as I always felt it wasn't treated as important as the other three gospels.

Mark's story tells of Jesus' ministry from his baptism to his death, burial, and the discovery of his empty tomb. It ends at Chapter 16 verse 8, the part read by Pope Francis at the Vigil. Mark's gospel does not tell a story of a miraculous birth or of post-resurrection appearances of Christ. Its author calls Jesus 'Christ' (meaning 'anointed one' from the Greek 'Christos' or the Hebrew 'messiah'). He is never referred to as God. It is only in Mark's gospel that we find Jesus referred to as 'the son of Mary' and called a 'carpenter' while the other gospels refer to him as 'the son of a carpenter.' For Mark's gospel, with no emphasis on a risen God, to be read at the Easter Vigil from the Vatican was surprising to me!

Mark's gospel has long been regarded by scholars as the most reliable of the four in its overall description of Jesus' life and ministry. Yet, in all four gospels, there is no mention of Jesus' life from about age twelve, teaching in the temple, until about age thirty when he shows up in Galilee. Where was he and what was he learning during those important years?

It seems to me that the masses don't require details, evidence, or facts if they are told what they want to hear and it can be assimilated into the collective mindset. Few seemed interested in knowing where Jesus was during those youthful years of his life, but I felt sure I was not the only one, in over two thousand years, who had the curiosity to ask the neglected question of Jesus' whereabouts during his youth. Since I was still a little hung up on where he was and if he was everywhere, I returned to my questioning. I was told, in a way that I should simply accept that Jesus spent those years working as a carpenter with his adopted father, Joseph. That answer always stirred doubt in me.

I know a number of carpenters who do great work, but there is nothing in their training or apprenticeship that prepares them for missionary work or teaching the good news. Usually, the best news they had to share was that the mitered joints fit perfectly. Perhaps that obtuse group of disciples were not curious enough to ask their teacher where he had been and what he'd been up to for the past fifteen years of his life. Perhaps he did tell them, and they had no idea of what he was saying.

Fortunately, I discovered others were interested in knowing more about Jesus and his whereabouts. For instance, Holger Kersten, in a well-researched and captivating book entitled: *Jesus Lived in India* (1983), chronicles the unknown life of Jesus (Yeshua), his travels, stays, and studies during those youthful years and following the crucifixion. Yes. I said 'following' the crucifixion. (I wondered if Father Wayward had read this book before I did.) As one might expect, a controversial and dangerous concept like this strikes at the heart of Christianity: The Resurrection. It seems we have put all our eggs in the basket of a Risen Jesus. Paul, the Christian persecutor and former Pharisee whose companion was Luke, a physician and New Testament contributor, assured us that without this belief in a Risen Jesus or His Resurrection, it's all for nothing!

What about Jesus' teachings? Was that all for nothing? It seemed it was what he was dedicating his life to— teaching a better way to live. Why not just keep vigilance over our daily lives and try to make each day a pleasant way to live? Stop the revenge, the hatefulness, and being afraid of everything and everyone. It seems that the Lawmakers had concerns with his teachings. He taught a better way to live: compassion, understanding, forgiveness, casting out demons (as were others at the time, like Muhammed), and Jesus even posed the question back to the Lawmakers confirming with them that their scriptures said, "Ye are all gods." Was he suggesting we could all be and do more because of the Christ within us? The messiah they awaited was within? They were not listening; they're not listening still…

Apparently, this rouge did not support the law of an eye for an eye. Nor was he a believer in stoning people to death. Forgiveness? Understanding? Fear not? What could these concepts mean when the law and the rule makers intend to keep you afraid? Wouldn't Jesus' teachings sound like those of an agitator? By his actions, wasn't he saying that the way we are living now is not a good way to live with one another in a society? I've never counted them but I know there are numerous times in the Christian Bible that Jesus is reported to have told us to not be afraid. Wouldn't those words anger those who want to keep you afraid?

Surprisingly, there are many people who call themselves followers of Jesus, Christians, and proclaim they trust in God but live every day in fear. Some of them even carry weapons because they are afraid and, by doing so, they create fear in others too. I don't know how, except through fear that, over time the instruction to 'turn the other cheek' became 'draw your gun first', or how that concept can be embraced by someone saying they follow Jesus. I believe the Christ in them knows the truth and the way.

Kerstens' book provides insight and a degree of clarity into Saint Paul's influence on Christianity for he had become one of the most important figures in early Christian history. Although Paul's conversion occurred more than a year after the crucifixion, Paul, a Pharisee and a persecutor of the disciples is the one who rises up to be their leader. It's told that Paul was struck blind by lightning or from staring at an eclipse of the sun, each a major event that, oddly enough, was not accurately recorded or reported. The

Good News reports that in that blinding moment, Paul heard Jesus' voice and only he understood what was said to him. He was blinded and could not see Jesus, but three days later a disciple of Jesus laid his hands on Paul's eyes and restored his sight. The author of these reports is thought to be Luke, the physician and companion of Paul. All Paul had to do then was get baptized, and he was 'in like Flynn'. A converted Pharisee to the movement. It seems to me that the disciples still could not recognize a man with a plan; or, at least, not understand the plan.

Since this event of Paul's conversion occurred more than a year after Jesus' 'death', and Holger suggests Jesus was living in the flesh in India at the time, I guess it's safe to say He is everywhere. As far as sightings and resurrections go, it might take forty days to prepare a caravan and even longer to travel to India. It remains, throughout time, that only those who seek to reconcile beliefs with facts or evidence will find the truth.

I believe if we are to evolve spiritually and be free, we need to do the work. There is no 'scapegoat'. Children can conger up scapegoats. To get out of trouble, they'll say their imaginary friend did the deed we caught them doing. Scapegoat is an idea and a word that came to us from the Jewish tradition where one could cast all their sins upon a goat and kill it, thereby symbolically killing off their sins in this sacrifice offered to their God. It is important to note this is symbolic, not a literal truth. This, like many earlier concepts and rites taken from former mythologies, became part of the newly formed religious sect, Christianity. I have never read or heard that Jesus announced that he would be the scapegoat for all who followed his teachings.

In the new religion, Jesus became referred to as the sacrificial lamb, who by his death and resurrection took away the sins of the world. Is this to suggest that Jesus is to blame for us not accepting responsibility for our thoughts and actions? Did He take away our free will; our choice? I don't believe so. Just the idea of Jesus, the Christ, as my 'scapegoat', makes me spin. It does not spin me like Dorothy, into the land of Oz. I already know that all I need is within me. It feels more like Lord Tennyson's 'faith in honest doubt' grabbing hold of me. As a believer in free will, in choices, I have to question, "What's up with this scapegoat concept?" If I can choose right or wrong and it makes no difference, then what is the purpose of free will? There are always consequences. It is wise to not deceive ourselves about that. We do have choices, and we will live and die by the choices we make.

The Christ in us will guide us if we ask for guidance and listen. My faith is strong that this energy of love and creation is in each one of us. Have a look inside. It's there somewhere. A crucifixion and resurrection should never deflect our focus from the teachings of Jesus and his purpose. My disagreeing with Paul does not make my faith meaningless or useless. I have faith that the divine is everywhere, and we can express that divinity in the world by our behaviors. If we trust in the divine and risk choosing a better way for ourselves, then, no doubt, God will surprise us!

I Have Decided

It will be tomorrow night. This is not because I want to give myself another day in case I change my mind, but because tomorrow is Hallowe'en. I have heard that on Hallowe'en night, the veil between this world and the next is very thin, maybe even opened. I might have a chance to slip through to the other side. After yesterday, I know the heat is back on. They might all think I'm stupid, but I've overheard enough of their closed-door meetings to know what's happening. They might have caught me in the washroom, but they have never caught me eavesdropping at the doors.

I know my brother will think I decided to do this last Spring when I was so scared and depressed. He didn't know why. My sister did but she didn't tell him. He's heard that once someone makes up their mind to suicide, their mood shifts and they seem happy again. It fools the people around them into thinking you're okay. That is not the case. I made no plan to die at that time.

It hasn't even been a year, more like six months, since that teacher heard all the noise and walked into the boys' washroom and caught me touching him. Before that, no one knew, and he couldn't tell anyone about me because he is what they call 'non-verbal' and very physically challenged.

He could not get out of his wheelchair. He needed my help to go to the washroom and to eat his lunch while he was at school. He made a lot of loud noises that most people got used to but he could not talk. It was getting near the end of the school year before summer break. They could have hung me out to dry then, but they didn't. I'm sure it wasn't to give me a second chance, as they put it to me. It was near the end of the school year, and school officials wanted to stay under the radar and avoid the wrath of the boy's mother, and of a community afraid to send their little ones to elementary school in the Fall because, in these small communities, the entire school may become suspected of housing child molesters.

If I lost my job, there might be rumors and whispers so, from the outside looking in, everything remained the same. In September, I moved to the Junior High School with my student to attend to his needs. I just had to promise to stop inappropriately touching this disabled and unconsenting boy and get some help for my desire and behavior, otherwise referred to as my 'problem.' While the meetings were taking place in May and June concerning me, I was terrified that I would lose my job, humiliate my family, and even be charged by the police if they became involved.

My student grew very disruptive at school. His mother was calling and wondering if there was a problem or any changes to his day as her son didn't want to leave the house in the mornings to go to school. She had been reassured that nothing had changed at school. That was true. There was one exception, however. My severely disabled student was now aware that someone else knew besides the two of us. His eyes saw what those other eyes recognized when we were caught in the washroom, but still, nothing changed. It is one thing when we can't help ourselves, but it is deeply devastating when others could help us but don't or won't. I couldn't help myself either. As sick as it sounds to some, there was an urge, a desire, and excitement that I found hard to control. I could quit my job, but I needed it. There was nothing else I could do. Until now, it felt safe.

His mother is complaining again. She says he had a great summer and, since September, has been very resistant and upset about having to go to school. He is fourteen now. It is becoming more challenging for her, as a single mom, to physically get him to go to school. She is demanding that the school provide additional services to help him with his anxiety.

In the past few weeks, a team of experts has been meeting with him at least twice a week, sometimes there are four of them with him, other times only two. They compare notes and discuss therapeutic options for him to try. There is a speech therapist, a social worker, a family support person, and a specialist who works with severely handicapped children. He has been assigned a special room where he goes a few times a day to be soothed. There is a combination of flashing lights, big colored disco balls twirling around the ceiling, and various beats of loud or soft music being played. Sometimes it is the loud music and certain colors flashing about the room that soothe him. At other times, it seems like none of it works. Sometimes he stares around the room wide-eyed looking terrified. The moans, groans, and loud sounds that erupt from him are completely ignored as if unheard. Perhaps those are his sounds joining in with the other sounds of music in the room. I don't know what the experts know, but it all seems chaotic. He never seemed soothed, just tired out.

One day I heard these experts in a private consultation wondering if maybe the student had been or was being sexually abused. There was concern expressed, but each one of them said they were not qualified to diagnose sexual abuse. The speech pathologist, whose work was mostly with the younger children at the elementary school, suggested the school psychologist be requested to see the student and offer her opinion. My student still couldn't tell her anything, but what if she thought sexual abuse was likely? Who would be the suspects?

It was three weeks ago when the principal asked me to come to her office. She wanted to know what was going on with me and if I was keeping my hands to myself. I lied that I was. She told me that I had to go see the psychologist as she was at the school once a week. I hadn't got any help for my problem yet so she was making sure I followed her demand for me to see someone. Now she had someone for me to see. She told me that she would know if I went because she would ask the psychologist herself if I had gone to talk with her. I didn't go to see her. Somehow I just couldn't tell her about it. She would probably have to report me. She would be the one who would have to blow the whistle on me; and tell the principal, the boy's mother, and the police. The ones who already knew would pretend they didn't know anything about it. She would be the 'troublemaker' and she didn't deserve that.

I knew the principal didn't like the psychologist because I had overheard things she had said to teachers about her. I don't know why she didn't like her though, but I overheard her tell them, "She wears her fuckin' heart on her sleeve." That seemed to bother her. I had a gut feeling that the principal wanted the psychologist to do her dirty work for her. The psychologist wouldn't be able to confirm from seeing my student that he had been sexually abused, but she would be able to confirm it if I confessed it to her.

Yesterday I saw the psychologist go to the principal's office door. She stuck her head in and said, "I heard you wanted to see me."

"Yes. Come in and shut the door," she was told.

The office blinds covering the window that provided a view of the hallway and stairs were closed. I approached the left side of the door. I heard the principal ask the psychologist if she knew me. I couldn't hear the reply. Her voice was much quieter. The principal continued with, "You must know his sister. She's a vice principal at one of your elementary schools. Have you ever seen such a weird family? There's a bunch of them; one's a dentist, one's a lawyer, one's a doctor, one's a teacher, one's a business owner, and then there's this guy! There is something wrong with him. I told him he has to go see you and talk to you about whatever his problem is. He acts weird. I don't know what's wrong with him, but I told him he's got to go see you and I want to know when he does. See if you can help him. And when he comes, I want you to let me know. I want to know what's going on with him!"

As I listened, I realized she was pretending she didn't know anything! She didn't tell the psychologist what my problem was, and it seemed like the psychologist didn't know. I heard her say, "Well, if he comes to see me, I guess he'll let you know himself."

"He has to come to see you, and I want you to tell me when he does because if he doesn't show up to talk to you in the next couple of weeks, I'll be calling him back in here."

The psychologist asked if there was anything else she wanted to talk about and was told that was the main thing. As the principal asked if everything was going fine at the school, I stepped away from the doorway. I was still at the entry to a corridor of classrooms when the psychologist came out of the office.

When we saw each other, I said, "Hi." She smiled. I said, "I was thinking I might stop by and have a talk to you one of these days."

She said, "Okay. Would you like to set up a time? I'm back here next Thursday."

I felt afraid and said, "No. I thought I might just stop by sometime."

Smiling, she said, "Sure. If I don't have a student with me, just come in." We both smiled and went our separate ways.

I got through today at school but I didn't sleep well last night. I don't think I'll sleep tonight either; I have so much on my mind. It doesn't matter though because after tomorrow night I'll be asleep forever. Yet my mind wonders what the principal meant when she said, "And then there's this guy!" I suppose she meant my family is intelligent, capable, and successful, except for me. She just sees me as someone with a problem who acts weird, and it doesn't bother her to tell other people that about me. Maybe, everyone thinks that about me anyway. I don't know why I even care. I guess I don't anymore. It's too late to care now.

I just know I am in deep shit and can't get out of it. I've lived here in our family home all my life and inherited this house when my parents died. I was born here and I'll die here.

At school, I had overheard some, mostly staff and teachers, call me a pervert, a child molester. Some have referred to me as gay or queer. I've tried for a long time to hide from myself and others. I never had a desire to molest children, and I never thought of my student as a child. He was a young man. I was his companion, his helper, his friend. I was the person intimately caring for him. Even with his severe disabilities, my affection for him grew. He became the one I could be myself around. It also felt like a safe secret for me. No one would know about us. Yet I was deceiving myself. I never wanted to look at the situation as me taking advantage of a helpless and unconsenting boy. It just seemed that if I kept it quiet, I could get away with it like so many 'normal' people with their wrongdoings.

I knew I could not let people know I was gay. A friend I knew back in my high school days was beaten to death because he was openly gay. Even today if anyone speaks of him, voices become a whisper, not because of the abuse and mistreatment he received, but to try to 'keep it quiet' that he was gay. I always knew, as I heard and observed, how homosexuality was looked down upon. Even the few gay couples who live in the area are spoken about in hushed voices accompanied by snickering. Simply for being who they are, gay men are taunted, disrespected, seen as not 'normal', and even physically abused or killed. I did not feel safe being myself, but who else could I be?

There were a few failed attempts for me trying to date girls. I never had that masculine bravado they seemed to be looking for. I never really had any guy friends who wanted to hang around with me. The ones I knew either had girlfriends or wives. One of those couples introduced Carla to me. They arranged for us both to come play cards at their house one night. It was a fun night and Carla and I kept seeing each other. Eventually, she moved in here with me; something of a convenience for both of us. People began to see and treat us as a couple. I tricked myself into believing that it was right for me because I could tell that others, especially my family, approved. Perhaps they were happy I was not alone; maybe even saw me as 'normal' when she and I were together. But Carla was never satisfied with me, and to be honest, I wasn't really happy living with a woman.

At first, I thought this must be what it is like in all heterosexual relationships and maybe that was why so many people cheated on each other. But if you are not with the right person who you feel fulfilled with, it's just two people making each other miserable. I'm glad she left me. I think she is happy now. It must have been ten years we were partnered; certainly long enough for me to be regarded and accepted as 'normal' in the community.

Tomorrow, I will get the rope from the shed and put it in the stairwell. I will keep the door to the upstairs closed until the kids stop trick-or-treating and coming to the door. It is usually all over by eight o'clock. I'm not leaving any note. I'll just play some music until I'm ready. I think my farewell song will be John Mayer's War of My Life… yeah, he sings my thoughts and feelings: *out of time and nowhere to run. I will have no more suffering, no more pain, never again.* (John Mayer, 2009).

A society that condemns homosexuality harms itself.
—James O'Keefe, MD. TedTalks, YouTube 2018, referencing the research of E.O. Wilson, Evolutionary Biologist

Felines and Felons

My friend and I were talking when a buddy of his saw us and came by to say hello. As they spoke, the name of a mutual associate came up. My friend remarked, "I haven't seen him in ages! The last time I saw him, he was going into the cat house down East." They both laughed and flashed glances at me. I smiled to be polite, having no idea what was funny. Later I asked a worldlier female friend of mine, "Is a cat house a place you go to get a cat?" She burst out laughing, but the surprised look intensified on her face as she realized I was serious.

She then said, "It's where you go to get a whore!"

Now, I was surprised. Apparently, a cat house is not where you go to get a cat!

Cats are often pawned off on you because your friend, neighbor, or relative had 'just one more left' in the litter, and had to find a good home for it. There are those cats acquired by the SPCA and are adopted out to people who want a cat to love. There is also the 'stray' who happens to hang around until it wins your heart. Some stores have cats for sale, and then there are the special breeds for the highbrow folks. These are produced under strict requirements. They are special and pricey! They don't necessarily do what you want them to do though. I don't know if a breeder's house is referred to as a cat house or not.

My friend Nora had one such special cat. A gigantic ball of grey fur with round blue eyes that would peer at you when you came to the door. Nora would always pick it up because she didn't want it to escape and get outside. She said it was a house cat. The cat was also aging, over fifteen years, at that time. Even as I entered the house, she would take the cat and put him in another room. It seemed the cat was a little territorial and only Nora or her husband, Rob, could manage its spontaneous and surprising behaviors. One evening when I was expecting them for a visit, Rob showed up at the door alone. I asked where Nora was. He said he had to drop her off at the General Hospital because the cat had attacked her. He insisted she would be fine, but that she'd likely be there for a while and he didn't want to wait around the hospital so he came by himself. He added she would need to get a Tetanus shot and some stitches as some cuts were deep.

My shocked look prompted him to tell me this wasn't the first time, and he didn't know why she kept that damn cat around. He indicated that she has had it so long there was no sense in getting rid of it now. Apparently, just before they were leaving, she picked up the cat to put it in another room before they opened the door. The cat objected.

Rob came inside and sat down to chat with my husband. I got him a drink because I needed one. All I could think was if Rob had clawed her, the police would be at their door tonight, but the cat would get away with it! A domesticated cat inside the home, attacking and injuring: Is this not domestic violence?

Late one Friday night when we were arriving at our cottage for the weekend, and just unlocking the door, my husband spied what appeared to be a small flashing light coming toward us. The outside light was on and the night was dark. It was when the small moving light approached the doorstep that we saw it was a cat. It stopped and looked at us. It had only one eye as the other was closed shut. We assumed it had been injured but healed over. We said hello to him and he came up the steps to greet us. My husband petted him and, like all cats seem to do when they greet me, he rubbed his body along my legs. I said, "Hello. I'm going to call you Wink because it looks like you're winking at me." He turned, went down the steps, and ran back toward the pond. When he looked back, his light still shone through that one eye. Then he seemed to disappear.

My husband laughed as I said, "Wink must belong to the Trolls who live under the bridge by the pond." As we went into the house, my husband seemed very happy to have had this greeting upon our arrival. It seemed so unusual that this cat suddenly came out of nowhere just to say hello and leave again. Every weekend for many weeks afterward it was the same thing. As soon as we got out of our vehicle, we would see him come running toward us. After welcoming us, as if to say he was glad to see us, he would run back toward the pond. The only time we ever saw him was just upon our arrival.

One Friday night, when we had grown accustomed to seeing him and looked forward to his greeting, he didn't show up. We were both worried. The following day, my husband was telling a neighbor how Wink didn't come to say hello last night. He was told that there had been an owl around and three cats went missing from the community over the past week. We assumed there were four that went missing. We never saw Wink again. It was almost as sad to lose him as if he had been ours to love for years.

Sometimes when children leave home and go out to live on their own, they decide they need a pet. A cat is often the pet of choice as cats don't need to be walked. You can also just leave their food and water out for them during the day, and they will eat when they need food. You couldn't do that with a dog, especially a Lab, because they will eat every morsel in the dish immediately and will check all day long to see if it's been replenished. Many places will not accept pets as residents. If your child needs to move to a new apartment and cannot take a pet there, the child will bring it home to Momma. This arrangement can work out well, and the parents will often fall in love with their little grand-cat, enjoying having it in their home.

Yet sometimes, and rather quickly, they come to realize they have inherited the Hellcat! The one who wants to sit at that sunny spot on the windowsill and does not like the plant or those sheer curtains and blinds in the way. If you are not compliant and pay attention to its messages to redecorate, your floor will be covered in potting soil and the cat will shred those window coverings in a matter of weeks. Your sofas and walls will suffer the same clawing and shredding until the cat has decorated your space the way it would like it to look. You will feel ashamed to have your friends in, and you may even decide: Enough! You will struggle and be scratched trying to put Sir Cat into the transport carrier to deliver him to the SPCA.

As a child, my recollection of removing unruly, or too many, cats was a variation of today's methods. Although adults still tried to hide from the children that they were getting rid of the cat or cats, the carrier was a burlap bag and the transporter was a local fisherman who was willing to take them deep sea fishing. As children, we got a walloping for our misbehaviors, but we knew we were deemed more valuable than cats because no one ever put us in a burlap bag. Even when there were a bunch of us! Children, today, are usually still held accountable for their misdemeanors. For instance, if an older child is reckless around the house and breaks a lamp, many parents will discipline them with the added requirement that the child replace the lamp. Now, you can dream all you want about the sights you'll one day see in this world, but I guarantee you this, you will never see a cat with a lamp over its back approaching the checkout at your local department store! And we have seen some sights there!

We would be outraged and punish and even ban family and friends from our homes if they came in and destroyed our property or attacked us. But not our cats! Their bad behavior is encouraged, like a spoiled brat who is laughed at and coddled and cleaned up after. Cats never have to take responsibility for anything! If you happen to ask, "What's new pussycat?" you will not hear the reply, "I took responsibility today!"

I have always found it surprising that there are so many men who love cats and either have them or want them. Maybe they want that greeting as they arrive home at the end of their workday; a furry, four-legged 'meower' who they believe is happy to see them because they don't know what those meows mean. I'll tell you. The cat is saying, "Where the hell have you been all day? Pick me up and caress me now!" No human could get away with that. But it seems men like hearing a meow. I am not recommending this as your neighbors may start calling your place a cat house. Perhaps the notion that a dog is 'man's best friend' has skewed my perception of reality; making me think men prefer dogs over cats. I really don't know of any cat who is willing to sit beside you all day long in the cab of your truck the way a dog will and look at you with eyes that say I am so happy to be here with you and mean it.

No! I don't know a cat that would even get into the truck. It would run and hide, or imply it had better things to do. I even thought that women prefer kittens or cats. But more and more I see that young women have dogs, not just as pets but as their protectors. A cat won't protect them! It will fend for itself. I am beginning to think that cats are just out for themselves and, on a whim, would even attack their owners if they displease them. A dog, however, is less likely to bite the hand that feeds it. If you have been kind to it, the canine wants to reciprocate. A dog wants to please its master. A cat does not have a master. It wants to please itself. However, if it serves their purpose, cats will lead you to believe you matter to them.

Angela had a cat for twenty-three years. She said it was a house cat because it didn't have claws. She was always trying to keep it inside but it insisted on trying to get out for a little fresh air. One day, it was faster than she was and got out the door. She screamed behind it, "Okay; go get yourself killed, see if I care!" A short time later, the cat returned and sat outside the door waiting for it to open. After that pussy enjoyed more freedom for she had taught Angela that just because she had no claws, she wasn't a house cat.

A friend and his partner were enjoying a warm summer afternoon in their backyard following his recent retirement. In an adjacent wooded area, they could intermittently hear a faint crying sound. This went on for a couple of days before they investigated. As they walked into the woods, the sound grew louder. Then, she saw it in some shrub. It was wounded, starving, and frightened. She ran to the house for a towel so she could safely capture it. Once she had it inside the house on a towel on the kitchen floor, she warmed some milk for it. The kitten soon accepted the milk. The vet was called. With an appointment secured, they drove to town to get kitty some medical attention. Its face and eyes were infected and the scars on its face and ears looked like they may have been made by a cat. My friend believed that an older Tom, perhaps its father, may have tried to kill the kitten. My friend, affectionately, named his new charge, Murphy, after some 'snaggle-puss', ugly, scared-faced character from a cartoon he watched on television. After paying the bill for inoculations, stitches, and medicine, they took Murphy with them to his new home.

It seems as though they and Murphy were destined to find each other. Seven years later, my friend talks about Murphy more than any of my female friends talk about their children or grandchildren. He 'complains' that the cat never bothers his partner, but that at five o'clock in the morning, it awakens him, purring loudly as it stands over his face and stares at him to get up. Apparently, his partner doesn't do that. Murphy would like to go outside for a while, or he'd like to play hockey. My friend cleans Murphy's litter box; sounds annoyed that when he gets up from the table this cat will attack him from behind. (Maybe acting out the role his cat dad played with him. Did he never wonder what might be in those genes?) He buys Murphy toys and feels the need to abruptly end our conversations because Murphy will not leave him alone until he goes and has a playtime with him. He ties a fishing bobber on a string and runs around the house with it for the cat to chase him. Seriously, how long would a child get away with that? I am inclined to think that if his child had asked him for a new toy, the child would be told no. The cat doesn't even have to ask!

A person, and many animals, whose lives you saved and to whom you gave care and nurturance, would be forever in your debt and hold you close in heart. Not a cat! In that language, cats only speak to humans, meows, it will look at you, and say; "So? I've got nine lives! And, by the way, the next time those guys in the big red truck come to get me out of that oak, tell them to bring a treat along. Do you know how anxiety-provoking that is?" They don't care what language you speak. They are only speaking meows. You, in your simple adoration, will be seduced by all those meows, and act like you are being courted by some Latin lover. The cat knows you will try to please. Your cat might also be curious enough to want to know, "Who was in charge before I arrived?" You won't understand a thing they are saying, but because you so adore them, you will pretend you know and you'll run to fetch a snack, get some milk, open the door, or grab a toy for it. If the cat is not interested or thinks you don't understand one single 'meow', it will snub you and walk away. If the cat decides it wants your company, it will curl up beside you and purr contentedly soothing you with its sound. When you pet it, a paw may reach to touch your face and, foolishly, you will think it is petting you too. In fact, it is depositing its scent on your face from the scent glands in its paw to tell you or anyone else, 'You're mine'! You don't own a cat; the cat owns you!

It is not my intent to make cats seem uncaring or insensitive. Years before Murphy was found, my friend had a black and white cat named Claw'd. At that time, he noticed there was a skunk hanging around the front door of their home. He saw it around the yard over several days. Thinking the skunk might spray its odor around their front entry, my friend decided he needed to get rid of the skunk. He is a man who owns a gun. He doesn't hunt and has never had cause to use this gun. Apparently, the skunk presented him with cause. The skunk was not guilty of anything. He simply evoked a fear of possibility. Now, I realize how tenuous some laws are, and recently heard that a young man, following a robbery, was charged with 'wearing a mask with intent.' Scared me! What do they call what I've been doing on Friday nights? Putting my make-up on and going downtown is clearly 'wearing a mask with intent'. I guess they just haven't caught me yet. Innocence seems subjective.

My friend got his gun out, loaded it, and went outside and shot the skunk. Claw'd was sitting there on the front step as he often did when his skunk friend came by to visit. Being a first-time shooter, my friend may have missed the skunk and shot Claw'd, in which case, I would not be telling this story. I would keep quiet and protect my friend, as I know there would be a posse of cat lovers on its way to find him. Yet, who is outraged by the death of an innocent skunk? The gun was put away, and my friend got a shovel and dug a hole in the wooded area to bury the skunk. He told me that Claw'd went to that burial mound and laid over it for several days. He said it wasn't until that moment that he realized he had killed Claw'ds' friend. He added, "I have never taken that gun out since." All the empathy is for the cat and its pussycat eyes.

Claw'd aged. My friend said he couldn't recall what happened to him. He assumed that Claw'd may just have gone away somewhere to die or, perhaps, something in the woods got him. I'd like to think Claw'd found a family of skunks who took him in to live with them. Or maybe, he just went to the cat house in the sky!

Erin, a young, independent woman I know with Down's Syndrome, lived alone and wanted a cat for company. I think Erin has a beautiful 'cat spirit' for she knows who she is and is proud of herself. If that makes others uncomfortable, that's their problem. Erin got herself a kitten. As a little girl, she had always had a cat. However, this one was never an affectionate cat although he would let you pet him, feed him, clean up after him, and pay his medical bills. He pretty much did what he wanted. He grew into an older cat and at age thirteen, developed diabetes. The vet said it could be managed and controlled with medication. Erin felt unable to manage this additional care by herself. It wasn't like this cat had been helping with the rent or anything. After much consideration, she made the difficult, but sensible, decision to take her long-time roommate to the SPCA. They would assess him and try to find a new home for him.

A few days later, Erin received a call from the SPCA informing her they would have to euthanize the cat. Erin was sad but understood. She was told that his age and medical issues were not the problem in finding him a new home, but those factors combined with his disposition made it very unlikely he would be adopted.

So, there you have it! If you are old and ill, you better be nice! This is no fable. It just seems to me that if you're a sour puss or can't be affectionate, you will not stand a chance. That goes for all you cats out there! 'Capisce?' 'Comprendez?' 'Entiendes?' 'Fahum?' Ah, to hell with it! 'Meow?'

Ravaged

I woke with a heavy heart this morning. As I lay in bed squinting at the brightness of the day, I reasoned this feeling was due to insufficient sleep although, when I first opened my eyes, it was already eight o'clock. Tossing and turning, unable to fall into my usual peaceful slumber last night seemed to be at the root of this tired heaviness in my body. No. There was more to it. It wasn't just my body. My whole being felt this weight and exhaustion. This was more about the events of last night. I began to wonder why I am attracted to men who are emotionally unavailable; whose love is unrequited. I flung the covers off me and got my feet on the floor before I went down that rabbit hole. Fully aware of the importance of asking myself this question, and equally aware that I needed coffee, I made my way to the kitchen.

There on the counter, just where we left them, were the empty beer cans and dirty glasses restoring my memory and ensuring I didn't escape my thoughts. I cleaned it up and made some coffee. Now I sit with this hot brew to reflect. These are not the usual thoughts that accompany my morning coffee. I would normally give thanks and think about my day ahead and what activities I'd engage in to create another pleasant day. Instead, my thoughts of last night pull me back. I resist. I know this feeling will take me to an inner darkness, but something deep inside beckons me there.

We met a few months ago through a mutual friend and had seen each other briefly a couple of times since then. We'd been texting for weeks and this past week he asked if he could come by for a visit as he would be in the area. It was wonderful to see him in person again. I nursed a rye and ginger while he told me about his work, and shared with me stories of people in his world, people I didn't know, but who were important to him.

He spoke of a veterinarian friend of his which led us to a discussion on pets and how they often seem more important than children to some people. I said, "People do love their pets."

He commented, "That's the only thing about the building I live in, no pets are allowed there. If I could, I'd have a cat."

Surprised, I said, "A cat? I would think you were a dog person." His glance told me there was something hurtful coming.

He said, "I had a dog when I was a kid. One day, my father and neighbor were walking over to his place, just down the street. The dog followed them; maybe jumping and nipping at them. He went in the house, got a gun, and came out and shot the fuckin' dog. That put me off dogs. I swore I'd never have another one."

It hit me hard. It was one of those times when it feels like you really feel another's pain. I told him something similar happened with me and cats. I was nine or ten and had just gotten a little angora kitten. It was a very rainy and windy Hallowe'en night, and I had gone out trick-or-treating with the other kids. My sister-in-law was there and she loved cats. I didn't worry about anything happening to it. When I got home, I asked where the kitten was. We looked around and couldn't find it. She said it must have run out the door when some of the kids left. It was pouring and I ran outside to look for it; to call for it. I couldn't find it and returned crying. My sister-in-law told me to stop. It was a cat and it would know to hide and stay safe. She said, "You'll find it in the morning." She was right. I did find it; drenched and dead in front of the garage door. I had to pick it up and bury it. My brother helped me. I swore I would never have another cat as long as I lived. In fact, I wouldn't go near one, not to pet or pick one up and hold it, for many, many years.

We both seemed to understand how hard it is to love when you know how easy it is to lose what you love. You can become so fragile. I noted that each of us had blamed the animal for hurting us even though the animals were innocent, just not protected. It may have been easier or wiser to blame the animals than to think we and our innocence might not be protected either. It's like one needs to blame the victims as a defense and protection from fear. If you are vulnerable, it's a matter of survival. No words confirmed this feeling, but it hung there in the air between us.

He was pouring his third beer when his memories carried him to his childhood and then forward again to his broken relationships. He glanced at me and said, "I don't know if you've ever read *Life with Billy*, but that's the story of my life; except my mother didn't kill my father. I don't trust anybody now. I just think everybody wants something from me. I guess that's what happens when you're five years old and you're trying to pull your father off your mother because he's beating the shit out of her, and then he beats you." Another glance at me as he continued, "I don't mean once or twice a year. This was almost a daily occurrence. It could go on every day for three weeks, then a reprieve for a week, and then another three weeks of it. My brothers and sisters were older; they would go and hide. I couldn't do that. I had to try and stop him every time."

"You were five years old," I said. "Your mother meant everything to you. You didn't want anyone to hurt her; especially your father. Of course, you'd try to help her."

He looked at me as I spoke and said, "Well, why didn't my brother? He's only three years older than me."

I suggested, "Maybe he did when he was five. You would have only been two. Maybe he later decided it was safer to try to protect himself."

He briefly studied my words, and then added, "Maybe. I don't know. We never talk about it."

It struck me how often we are silenced by shame and grief; yet we wrap it like a protective blanket around our love for one another. Keeping silent about our emotions with those who, we know, share in them in some way, but whose personal experiences we can't bear to hear or carry on top of our own. It's as if the sharing might solidify a sense of combined helplessness that would be unbearable: The notion of not being able to help myself, and not being able to help you.

I realized I had, unknowingly, reached out and put my hand on his arm while he spoke about this painful memory. He didn't flinch or shrug my hand off. He allowed me to touch him. Yet, I had caught a look in his eyes when he glanced at me. In these morning reflections, a movie I loved just flashed into my mind. It was Biscuit and the scene was when, after much resistance, Biscuit allowed a moment of physical connection with the one trying to tame him. I could recall seeing in the horses' eyes a wanting to be sure it was safe to trust. That was the look I had seen in his eyes last night.

My thoughts drift. I recall back to the moment of him apparently thinking about addictions. Abruptly, he turned to me and questioned, "What is an addiction anyway? Why do some people have them?"

To my surprise, I answered, "I think everyone has an addiction to something: substances, gambling, sex, drugs, self-sabotage, even putting others first all the time. For me, an addiction is anything we give our power to repeatedly. The thing we cannot say no to." It appeared our conversations had been intense, and had brought about a catharsis of some kind for him. A moment of comic relief was due.

He half smiled at me and said, "Well, what about Mrs. Whitten? She was a really nice lady. A very private person. I used to do some work for her: mowing, shoveling, and stuff like that. What was her addiction?" Without anticipating a reply, he answered himself, "Oh, I know! It would have been Tooney Tuesday at Kentucky Fried Chicken. She loved Tooney Tuesday at KFC."

I took Billy Joel's advice and left *a tender moment alone.*

He got up and said he had to go for a smoke. He turned to me and said, "I hope I can come back, can I?"

I answered, "I hope you do."

He wasn't gone long; just long enough for me to refresh my drink, and for him to smoke half a cigarette. When he got back, he locked the door behind him, poured himself another beer, and sat down beside me. He took a sip of the beer and said, "I shouldn't have poured that. I'm not going to drink it. If I do, I'll be drunk." He sat it back down on the sofa table.

He began telling me again how he didn't trust anyone; how he believed that if anyone could like him, it must just be because they wanted something from him. It stung. I was hearing a belief from him that I once told myself about myself. It was that notion that anyone who was kind to you was only using you. No discernment. No way, yet to figure out who, if anyone, could be trusted. I felt wounded by his self-deprecation as if he was telling my life with his words. It hurt to hear him tell himself a lie. The same lie I once told to myself. I knew any comments I made would feel like platitudes and bullshit to him.

I remained silent as he told me about some of his failed relationships. The German girl, Ana, a love that faded and was pretty much over within its fourth year. Sherry, for whom I sensed there remained a fondness by his smile when he spoke of her; and Kim, a connection, a live-in, someone with whom he had learned some things. It seemed he had already decided that he wouldn't love or trust anyone.

Maybe he just couldn't love or trust. Maybe he didn't know what it was like to love or trust anyone.

I considered a truth I have come to understand and accept. There are only two forces to guide us: love and fear. They cannot occupy the same space. Where there is love, there is no fear. If fear is ruling and guiding, there is no love. If love is stronger, fear will surrender to it. I considered that perhaps there was no love in the fearful world he lived in, and he was only guided by fear.

It seems that for nearly all my life, I had only dated men who were either emotionally immature or unavailable. I have wondered from time to time if I could ever attract an attentive, committed man.

Last night I listened to this man and his self-whipping and distorted honesty. In the strangest of ways, I felt privileged to hear it. He told me how he had been rejected over and over again, and how after a while, "You give up trying to be in a relationship because you're protecting yourself from being rejected."

It was then I made the mistaken offering of saying, "You need to learn to love yourself first."

He turned toward me, and with a controlled anger in his voice, said, "I don't need to do anything. It really pisses me off when someone tells me I need to do something! I don't need to do anything but breathe and eat."

I managed to say, "You don't need to do anything for anyone else, but you do need to do that for yourself."

He repeated, "I don't need to do anything but eat and breathe."

He said, "If you and I were dating, and I saw you look at another man, that would be it!"

I heard myself whisper, "I wouldn't." He heard it, too, and glanced at me.

He continued, "I know it's crazy; I know it's wrong; I know it makes no sense. I know it's not fair, but that's how my head works. I'd tell myself that you want him more than me because he's stronger, smarter, better looking, whatever I can think of. I'd tell myself, 'Why wouldn't she want him over me because I'm nothing.' I'd always be waiting and watching for that moment you fuck up!" I wouldn't call his honesty wholesome, but it provided clarity.

He had no idea how much it hurt me to hear him say those things. I wondered about my own feelings. Was I interpreting his remarks as an insult to my judgment? Was it a reminder of my own low self-esteem and a need for me to still work on overcoming rejection? How many women have loved him that he felt rejected by, only because he wouldn't love himself; because he wouldn't see his own worth? It could be seen through the eyes of others I realized as he spoke about some of the sweet comments his lovers had said to him. I was torn to understand if he knew on some level they were true or if he was just amused by them. I hoped he knew those honest and kind insights about him were true and that he was only holding those truths outside his defensive wall.

Now, this morning, I wonder about my own self-worth. I know I deserve better than what he was dishing out, but is there something in me that thinks I can help self-loathers, the emotionally needy, those who have turned their own suffering into an abuse of others through manipulation to simply get what they want? The role of a victim may just be the card he plays to needy but kind-hearted women, who he believes want to rescue him, if only for the night. But he still carries a hatred and loathing like a defenseless victim. Some experiences provide insight into ourselves, yet we are often non-reflective and miss the opportunity for self-growth.

Without sentimentality, I wondered if he had ever looked into his own eyes, into that window to his own soul, and seen what attracted love to him. He didn't seem to know that others were drawn to a goodness they detected in him; to a soul that inherently knew right from wrong and had known it all his life, to an honesty that would fight for what's right and for the innocent and helpless. He might prefer to believe that it was the 'poor baby' or 'little victim' he expressed about himself that was what attracted the feelings and compassion of others. Although he may think he had overcome his loss of innocence and helplessness and the hurt within him, he did not realize it was evident to the discerning soul. Manipulation of others is not compassion for oneself, and without compassion for himself how would he have the fullness of life and love he deserved? I had the sense that when he recognized someone's attraction to him, he made it his duty to inform them of who he believed he really was.

Even his 'fair warnings' seemed like a sign of his compassion and consideration of others, but not of himself. It was as if he felt compelled to tell of his abusive childhood as if to create an intimacy with you. Something that would not be shared with everyone. He reveals how his self-identity developed as someone who was less than everyone else and was not worthy of being loved.

Yet, those experiences did not form his identity; they formed his belief about his identity. That is something that could be and needs to be changed because it is false. If fighting, quarrelling, hurting, running away and unfaithfulness were all he had ever known about personal relationships, it could make sense why he did not want anyone to fall in love with him. He said he hated to fight, but he fought hard with himself to maintain the integrity of his false identity. He chose to act in ways that solidified his belief. He wanted to hold fast to that self-deprecation. From a child-like perspective, he claimed his mastery of self-preservation not realizing, as an adult, it was nothing more than his own self-punishment and abuse which still deprived him of the love he was born to know. By his beliefs, he continued the parental abuse on himself.

It makes me wonder what kind of defeat a child experiences when its own inner knowing fails to convince adults of a better way to behave; when the power resides in the weakness of adults and not in the strong survival instincts and inner knowing of the child. To me, it feels like an assault on our very existence, our right to be here and to be confirmed as worthy. It is certainly a model that teaches abused children how to behave in relationships by simply taking what they want and giving nothing in return.

I recall the look on his face last night when he told me that he was nine or ten years old when he was playing with a couple of neighborhood boys. He innocently asked them, "How often does your dad beat you?" He paused, looked at me, and said, "That was when the light went on. They both looked at me shocked and confused and said, 'Dad doesn't beat us'." He continued, "I was just as stunned as they were.

But I knew then that not everybody lived as we did. That was the turning point in my life." He added that he loved school; "Not because I was any good at it but because I felt safe there." He became involved in sports, doing jobs for others, helping out to get some money, and to stay away from home. He said eventually his mother left his father and took them away from there. She worked for years until her legs gave her so much trouble that she couldn't stand all day at her job. He said he then worked three jobs to support himself and her; to take care of her.

I asked, "Why didn't your siblings help out?"

He answered, matter-of-factly, "They were gone. When you grow up in an alcoholic family, you get out of there as soon as you can." He said he was forty years old before he forgave his father, but added he hadn't fully forgiven him; only partially. He said he didn't think he would ever fully forgive him.

I said, "Forgiveness is for you, not him."

He looked at me and said, "I don't want to let go of it. I want to remember." He didn't realize how deeply I understood the concept of wanting to remember. But forgiveness is not forgetfulness. It is helpful to remember what we have forgiven so we are not caught in a cycle of abuse where our forgiving becomes our self-abuser. I believe that forgiveness requires us to move on, not forget.

It's very peculiar how some of his responses to his life experiences seemed so similar to mine although his experiences were very different. Well, different in details, but similar at the soul level where the wound is deepest; where we have been ravished. Even when some wounds have a physical appearance, that is not the extent of the wound. All abuse causes an emotional wound that is internal, and often slow healing.

I've heard it said that opposites attract, and I've heard it said that like attracts like. What should I believe? I wonder what it is in me that attracts these undesirable men, or what it is in them that attracts me to them. I stopped dating for a long time and even sought therapy on this journey of self-discovery. During that time, I had a dream of a man who was a composite of several men I knew. In the dream, I was making bread for him. I saw him approach me with an intense scowl on his face, yet I smiled and said to him, "I love everything about you!" His look said he didn't believe me and that I couldn't possibly love everything about him. Suddenly, I woke and I knew I didn't love everything about him. I was lying to him. Why did I say that to him? In the dream, it felt like I was genuinely expressing my feelings, but in reality, I did not like many of the characteristics of the men who comprised my dream man. I knew he was a symbol of my masculine energy that was somewhat flawed and whose development and maturity seemed arrested.

Usually, mentally arrested development occurs when a person is unable or unwilling to take care of an emotional vulnerability they have experienced. They may be 'unable' if they are emotionally vulnerable at a very young developmental stage. However, to be 'unwilling' to deal with emotional vulnerability later in life is often a conscious decision that denies the problem, or wants to hold on to it for some reason. From my dream, I recall wondering why I had accepted and loved this underdeveloped part of myself. Did I think that making bread (a symbol of life itself, and one connecting us to basic emotional and biological satisfaction), and loving all the disdainful parts of him was appropriate? Was this masculine energy annoyed that I was ignoring my truth, and not doing the real work to help my masculine side to mature? Recalling that dream reminded me that last night I was still drawn to aspects of this immature masculine. Obviously, I have more work to do.

Where do we learn of the strong, positive traits of masculinity? Have we known people in our lives that we've been close to who have demonstrated leadership, emotional strength, courage, and respect for the feminine? Is the lack of a role model the reason we don't develop mature masculine energy?

What stands out for me and seems common in our wounds is the early awareness; a knowing, not an understanding, that informed us both at a very early age. The incongruence between what we knew and what we witnessed in adult behavior around us. Both of us developed a hyper-vigilance to our environments, and to this day, remain acutely aware of the movements, the sights, the smells, the sounds, the words, and the tones, the glances of everyone and of everything around us. The carnage of distrust. It creates the need to keep one's world and environment safe. It seems that we both got pretty good at pretending to tune things out and appear at ease in our environments.

As we age and try to cope with all we are presented with in life, we can and do learn to discern who and what we will trust. For the most part, we've figured out *when to hold 'em, fold 'em, walk away, or run.* Any misjudgment we make in this regard can send us spiraling until we can regain control. I recall hearing him sing those lyrics when he was in the kitchen pouring a beer. They are words that obviously resonate with him.

It's uncanny how we have both been nurturers of others and somehow unwittingly, hoping that the care we gave would be reciprocated by someone who would love and nurture us someday. Part of our problem arises when we are nurtured and cared about, but we don't trust it. We think there's a hook. We tell ourselves, 'If they really knew what I'm like, they wouldn't love me'. Then, we do all we can to prove ourselves right, and chase the love away; reaffirming to ourselves that we really are as worthless as we keep telling ourselves we are. What we believe is true; as long as we believe it. When we change our beliefs, we change our lives!

I refresh my coffee as I remember the day my light went on. I think I was in my mid-forties: going through 'a dark night of the soul'. I was receiving some gratitude and praise from people for some things I had done. This was coming from several sources in a short period of time. The common message I heard was how much I had helped them and how grateful they were to have me in their lives and that I had made a positive difference for them. I was gracious, but felt they were all just being polite to me; that it was all just a facade. Instead of lifting my spirits, it took me to a dark, unconscious place. I heard my own voice asking me, "If you're so good at nurturing and taking care of everybody else, why don't you take care of yourself? Who do you think is going to come along and nurture and care for you?"

I even heard the answer: "Nobody."

The experience surprised me. I questioned where it was coming from. I felt loved. I knew I was loved by my family and friends. I felt respected and appreciated in my career. Why did I feel I needed nurturance and care? I did give a lot to those I loved. It was the way I had learned to be. If those I cared about seemed unappreciative or acted like my actions or support was not enough, then I'd give more. If they hurt my feelings, I'd forgive them more. As I began to examine my life, I immediately saw a little girl who was sad or serious too often; who didn't giggle or play silly like other children did; a little girl who made sure she did everything asked of her, and did it well so she would get some praise and wouldn't get 'into trouble' (meaning she wouldn't get punished for being less than perfect).

I saw a child who grew into her teens feeling distrustful of many of the adults in her world, every moment was spent in heightened awareness of what they were doing or saying; like an animal sniffing out traps. Today, as an adult, there are still people I know who trigger those feelings in me when I'm around them. Now I respond better, for I have learned the problem with always having your guard up is that it is inappropriate when you are in a safe and loving place. My instincts have taught me to recognize the truth in the moment.

One day, I took a good look at myself in the mirror; I looked myself straight in the eyes. I told myself what I loved about myself; why I was a good and worthy person. I acknowledged my weaknesses and my flaws. I accepted them as part of me. Everyone has his or her own special strengths and weaknesses. Mine are my very own. They make me who I am. I am okay with that. It's called acceptance. For me, I need to be and do my best. I believe if I can be my best self, I will be giving my best to others. What more could I give them?

As I continued to reminisce, I remembered that during my self-examination that day, I had suddenly recalled my older brother who, at age fourteen, had announced he was his own boss. Although I was much older than fourteen on my day of reflection, I decided it wasn't too late for me and I, too, would be my own boss. After all, who else can be my boss without me giving my own power over to them? I grew strong that day.

While I sit here this morning, my thoughts and recollections keep bringing the past forward. This is what he was doing last night.

Following his smoke break, our conversations continued. He had things on his mind, things he wanted to say. Truths, confessions, his reality, his decency, and his need to not mislead me. His urge to make sure I understood that 'he was not worthy'. The longer I listened, the closer I felt to him. I had long ago outgrown judgments. I have grown in confidence and trust in myself and in what I see and experience. If my intuition and experience align, I will not accept anything I am told to try to convince me otherwise. Doubting myself is no longer an option for me. I admit, I have been disappointed; maybe even a little heart-broken at times, but I am not devastated. I will not deny the truth of my experience because someone else refuses to face their own truth. They will have to own that. It is not mine.

I think now about how I reached to embrace him. He turned and held me. We kissed. He asked if we could cuddle on the bed. I knew he meant more than cuddle. I also noted that he has a tendency to not ask for what he really wants. I think my awareness of this was peaked from the story he told me about his mother. She would call and ask him what he wanted for dinner and he would say 'porridge' because he knew that is most likely what they would have to eat. He said his mother would tell him not to say that in case someone overheard him. It struck me how that is a strategy children learn as a way of not being disappointed. Don't ask for more than you think you'll ever get.

I got up and led him to the bedroom. He seemed to be instantly naked and then undressed me. Our passion quickly escalated. His gentle touch and passionate kisses soon grew into a hurried roughness; not the love-making of a man who can taunt you and take you to the brink of ecstasy, or who wants that done to him. He became like a zealous young man in his passion for self-gratification, unable to withhold himself any longer.

As I lay there in his arms afterward, I said to him, "From what you told me, it sounds like I can never win your heart."

He answered, "I wouldn't say never, but it would probably take a long time." I was silent, but thinking, *neither of us has a long time. We are both well past the prime of our lives. All we have is now. We can choose it to be a now unencumbered by the past, and unafraid of the future. A present moment of giving and receiving passion and love.* That, too, may be ravaging.

As I sit here, this bright sunny morning, reflecting, I think about the Norman Rockwell picture that hangs in my front entry. It carries the caption, 'Do Unto Others As You Would Have Them Do Unto You.' The Golden Rule. Treat others the way you want to be treated. I wonder if his words to me last night were inspired by that picture. He had said to me that his plan is to do unto others before they do unto him. Not Golden! A plan born from an idea, a thought, a belief that you will hurt me, but I will hurt you first. I smile at the irony. In truth, we are already hurting ourselves first by not allowing love in or by being cynical of love. I think what he really means is 'I'll hurt myself first before I'll let you hurt me'.

It is true that when someone rejects our love, we can feel hurt because we often hope for love in return. Generally, people do not want their love to be unrequited. But love itself asks nothing in return. It is unconditional. It seems to me that if I feel love for someone, there is nothing they can do about it if my love asks nothing in return. It may be that only unconditional love can ravage fear.

Where Did You Learn That?

There are so many things we learn in life and we are not consciously aware of learning them. But children, sometimes through their behaviors, their speech, or their play, can and will reveal to us what they have been learning. I'm not telling you what that is about right now. This is not your Coles notes. You have to read the whole story. Schooling, that formal setting of getting an education, required the student to pay attention and be aware of the lessons they were being taught. Most of us could write the full contents of what we learned from those formal engagements on the back of a cigarette package if we still had one. But the important lessons we'd need to know, those moments that caught our attention and branded the experience and memory into us; those are the real influencers of our lives.

Like the day Mama needed to bake bread and we had no yeast. Our mother could make several loaves of bread and a pan of rolls for the same coin that could buy a couple of yeast cakes or one loaf of store-bought bread. Besides, we'd need several loaves to feed us all. Mama sent my brother, a year and a half my senior, to the store for yeast. He was about seven years old. There were lots of safety instructions given and plenty of looks out the windows during the twenty to thirty minutes he was gone. Then, we saw him coming safely up the gate lane with the brown paper bag swinging in his hand. There was happiness in his return and relaxation in Mama's voice when she heard that everything went alright. Before he handed the bag over to Mama, he reached inside and took out his chocolate bar. Whenever anyone went to the store, if there was a nickel or a few cents left over after the purchase, it was treat-money for the person completing the mission.

My eyes grew large when I saw the candy bar. I asked him, "Can I have some?"

My brother clenched his chocolate bar close to his chest, turned his back to me, and said, "No!"

He headed toward the living room and I turned, whining to Mama, "He won't give me any!" She told me to hush.

She lifted her voice, telling my brother, "Come here." He returned to the kitchen with only the first bite missing from his candy bar.

She asked him, "Could Mama have a little piece of your chocolate bar, please?" She knew he wouldn't refuse her, but the look in his eyes showed disbelief at her asking the question. He hesitated as if to give her time to rethink what she was asking. I heard her say, as she bent toward him, "Just give me a little piece." He broke off a bite-size piece and gave it to her. She thanked him and told him what a good boy he was for sharing. He seemed happy, but he didn't waste any time turning and going in the other direction to be alone with his chocolate bar. As soon as he was out of sight, Mama passed me the piece of candy and firmly told me, "Keep quiet about it." I smiled, said thank you, and savored that piece of candy. I would not betray her. She has been dead for sixty years now, and I just recently let our secret out to my brother. I know she would laugh to think I wouldn't 'tell on her' all those years.

It was an important lesson for a child to witness who held the power, and how it could be used to bring about peace and maintain it, keeping all parties happy and satisfied in the process. When you earn and hold that status of respect, trust, and fairness, you know you can make requests and get results that others cannot.

By the time I was eleven years old and in grade six, I didn't have to ask for chocolate bars anymore. There was a new family who had moved to our consolidated school area in time for September classes. There were three children in their family, one in each of the three classrooms shared by students from grades K-2; 3-4 and 5-6. The oldest child, Wayne, was in my class. By the end of September, I began finding chocolate bars inside my desk after recess at least once or twice a week. The first bar I found made me double-check to make sure I was at my own desk, and that no one had moved the desks around. It was mine. My scribblers, my books with a chocolate bar laid on top. As the kids assembled to their seats, I asked if anyone was missing a chocolate bar because I had found one inside my desk. No one claimed it, and someone said they guessed it must be mine then. I knew it wasn't so I left it there until the end of the day. When no one had claimed it, I ate it on the walk home from school. This was not a one-off.

Bars began appearing inside my desk, usually on Monday or Tuesday and always on Thursday. Some kids would have money to spend at the canteen across the road, and if they were bus students, they would go there at recess or lunchtime. No one would own up to being my chocolate purveyor. By mid-October, I had been trained, and I was beginning to look for and expect a chocolate bar. I didn't care if anyone ever admitted putting them inside my desk. One day, while sharing a bar with one of my school friends, I jokingly commented that I was getting a little tired of wafers and malt and was wishing for something with more caramel and nuts. Apparently, word didn't get back to the source, and I continued to get the same kinds of chocolate bars until the day of revelation. It was a Friday afternoon, just before the weekend, when those 'types' always delivered their unwelcome news.

A grade-five student came up to me and called me aside. She had a secret to tell me. She whispered that she knew who was putting the chocolate bars inside my desk. She had seen him do it with her own eyes as if to assure me she had not seen him with someone else's eyes. As I listened to her, I began to think what a sly little snot she was for spying. If I wanted this mystery unraveled, I could have spied myself. I felt an urge to tell her to shut up. But while I was deliberating on what to say to her, she was out with it! "I saw Wayne putting a snack bar into your desk yesterday at recess."

All I could utter was, "Why didn't you tell me sooner?" She said she didn't have a chance. I thanked her but was thinking: *That's right; you don't have a chance. You're pathetic.* Wayne was not in school on Friday.

At least, I had the weekend to consider how I would approach Wayne on this delicate matter. I decided I would have a talk with him on Monday before I went home for lunch and before he went to the canteen. After recess on Monday, there was a chocolate bar awaiting me. I noticed it, left it there, and decided to give it back to him at lunchtime. As soon as the bell rang, I took the bar and went to Wayne's desk. Suddenly, the little grade-five spy was standing beside me. I said, "Wayne, I know it was you who has been putting the chocolate bars inside my desk." Wayne looked surprised, laughed, and denied it. Little 007 showed no fineness and would have no banter. She blurted out her accusation and stood very close to me as if we were blaming him together.

I told Wayne I really appreciated and enjoyed all the candy bars but I didn't want him to keep spending his money on me. In his innocent and careless confession, he assured me he didn't mind spending his money on me and he wanted to do it. I then told him my backup plan which I thought up on the weekend. I said, "I can't eat too much candy because it's giving me blemishes." I passed the bar in my hand to him and said, "Here, you keep this one."

He said, "No. No. It's for you. You keep it." I resisted. He insisted.

Finally, I said, "I'll keep it if you promise me you won't buy me any more bars." He promised. I guess 007 had lost interest or was called to another assignment as she had disappeared. But there was still a mystery I wanted solved. I turned back to Wayne and asked, "Is snack bar or malted milk your favorite bar?" He said neither one was his favorite. I asked. "Did you think they were my favorites?" He said he didn't know, but every time he went to buy me a Crispy Crunch or an O Henry, they were sold out before he got there. I smiled at him; satisfied. At least he had tried.

Wayne was a boy of his word. He never did buy me another chocolate bar. I wasn't too concerned because I knew Hallowe'en was only ten days away.

I do hope Wayne learned a lesson though. If a guy wants to catch a girl, he should invest in the bait she likes. A few O Henry's might have made the difference. I feel confident there would have been more mileage in that even with spies lurking about.

By the time the Christmas break was over, I was taking more interest in moving on to Junior High. Each day, I was excited for my brother to get home on the school bus as he was in grade eight, and the stories he had to share were always astonishing and made me giggle. I could hardly wait to go to his school.

My brother seemed to be in a classroom with a band of mischiefs. There were at least three names I recall him mentioning; Stu, Wally, and Brent. I think the term he used for them was 'the classroom clowns.' It appeared they were not classroom learners as they seemed to have a much more 'hands-on' approach than just holding a pencil.

In those days, students stayed in their classrooms and teachers moved from class to class. Mr. Comeau, an able-bodied, athletic man, who had only one arm and no tolerance for disrespect, taught in English but with a strong French accent. On several occasions, he had to put disruptive students, namely Wally and Stu, out of the classroom. When he had enough, he would tell them, 'Take the door', meaning 'get out'! They were not allowed to remain in the class. This occurred more than once. The intelligence, wisdom, and ingenuity of these boys were evident to some teachers, and they seemed to have more leeway or tolerance in some classes. Then came the day when Mr. Comeau again told the boys to 'take the door'. They obeyed him.

Like synchronistic demons, they approached the door, removed the bolts, and took the door with them. Even the most frightened student was surprisingly amused, as was Mr. Comeau. Those two boys carried the door partway down the hall, got a few laughs, and returned the door to its proper place. They were then told to visit the principal's office where they explained their presence to him. The boys had done their prep work at lunchtime in anticipation of what was likely to happen in their upcoming class.

Then there were the Brent stories. He seemed to be an independent actor. Some students had no interest in learning a second language. They barely had command of their first. Brent was one such student who was not very interested in learning French and was generally not attentive in class. I once heard his French teacher described, by a friend of my brother, as having thick lenses in her glasses and her slip was always hanging well below her hemline. In the early sixties, it was still something most women felt bashful about, having their slip or undergarment showing. This display was a regular occurrence for this French teacher and, to some, it seemed she had no shame. Such nonsense was later debunked by a younger group of feminist women who either threw their slips away or turned the look into a fashion statement of layered flounces. There are only solutions! However, cultural expectations are subtle and influential and some will cling to them.

Over the weekend, Brent had found a pair of glasses with thick lenses and brought them to school on Monday.

The kids called them Coke bottle lenses because of their thickness. They magnified his eyeballs when Brent wore the glasses. They had also been someone's prescription glasses and were a strain on his eyes when he had them on for very long. Nevertheless, Brent was in the mood to create some of that strange mimicking kind of fun; the kind that can border on hurtful when it gets turned into making fun of someone.

Brent sat in French class and put on the eyeglasses. He then turned and looked at the other students and got them giggling at the magnification of his eyeballs. When he tried to remove them, the teacher made him put them back on thinking his sight must have been very bad for him to need such strong corrective lenses. She was required to wear similarly strong corrective lenses herself. It was near the end of class when he could no longer tolerate wearing them, but since the teacher insisted he had to finally tell her that they were just a pair he found and had put them on for fun. She took them from him and broke them into two. The fun was over.

It was in May of that school year when the grade six students from all the elementary feeder schools went to the high school for their grade seven orientation day to prepare them for their Fall transition. I was excited to go to my brother's school.

The school day was almost over, but the bell had not sounded. I wanted to swoop by my brother's grade eight classroom hoping to get a look at some of the characters he had told me stories about. They were like living legends to me, and I wanted to see them in person.

Suddenly, there was a loud cheering and thunderous applause coming from my brother's classroom as I neared it. Then the bell rang. Students from the grade nine class across the hall came pouring out through their door, also curious about the loud applause. We all watched as the grade eight classroom door opened and students began to stroll out wearing smiles and pleasantly chatting with one another. The questions were fired at them. "What's all the noise about?"

"Why were you guys clapping?" The answer I heard was even more astonishing.

Almost simultaneously, two students replied. "Ralph knows his ABC's!"

"Ralph can say the alphabet now!"

There was no humor or sarcasm detected as I scanned the faces of Ralph's classmates who were emerging from the classroom. The looks and energy around me were of pure pride! Although I was struggling with my disbelief that Ralph did not know his ABCs before this, I could understand why everyone was so happy for him. He was a really nice guy! He used to go to my school one time. He was a gentleman, respectful, pleasant, and always had a kind word and a greeting for everyone. He was never a scrapper or shit-disturber. He was always considerate of others. If you disliked Ralph, there was something wrong with you.

As I watched the activity around me, tried to process what I'd heard, and took note of the faces who were recognizing a new student in their midst, my brother came out of his classroom. I approached him with a 'Hi' and asked him to point out Stu and Wally for me. He looked around the hallway and back into the classroom. He said, "They must have already gone. They're not here." My heart sank. I had been so distracted by the news about Ralph that I had allowed myself to lose focus on my mission. I would have to wait until September before I'd catch a glimpse of them.

As I boarded the bus, I took a seat alone. This was good because I needed time for reflection. On the drive home from school, I wondered how Ralph made it to grade eight without knowing the alphabet. How could he read and write and do the assignments all those years? It must have been so hard for him. I wondered if anyone helped him with his schoolwork. I thought about his dedication, and that this was the day he had achieved his goal, something he must have wanted all these years. School was not hard for me. Although I did the work and put in the effort, my awards, achievements, and high honors seemed insignificant now. Ralph had shown dedication, commitment, and real determination in his learning process, and he had reached a goal that many have never had to work that hard toward. He didn't take his eyes off the prize, and today he was victorious. He had the courage to never give up on himself. What arose in me was pride in Ralph. I felt I understood and shared in what his classmates had expressed earlier; an overwhelming pride and joy for him. He possessed the qualities of a hero.

I thought about an experience I had a couple of years earlier when a cousin, Greg, had stopped by our home one Saturday morning for a visit. He had been hitchhiking and came in to see my brother, Dave, who was just getting up. Greg sat on the chair, picked up the newspaper, and began reading it. I believe I had heard, somewhere along the way that he had been expelled from school in grade two for his many 'misbehaviors'. He was punished and sent home where he was punished again. It was a few years later when a doctor diagnosed him with epilepsy. This was finally controlled for him with medication. Greg never returned to school but stayed home to help on the farm. On that summer morning, I recall my brother asking him why he was reading the newspaper. Greg answered, "So, I'll know what's going on in the world. That's why I taught myself to read." I recalled taking notice of that and was impressed. Both Greg and Dave were about sixteen years old at the time. Dave said he was going to go have a smoke. Greg looked over the top of the newspaper and said, "If God meant for you to smoke, he'd have given you a chimney!" I grinned then just as I was grinning on the school bus thinking, Greg, too, was pretty smart and funny.

I believe it was Mark Twain (aka Samuel Clemens) who said that those who don't read have no advantage over those who can't read. On that grade seven orientation day, the only thing I learned or recalled was that both Ralph and Greg had achieved an advantage over many by their sheer determination and conviction that they could do it. Just like the little engine! It wasn't easy for them, but they did not give up on themselves. That was a really worthwhile lesson those guys taught me.

September came and I was bussed to my new school. I hung out with some old school friends and met some new ones who were my classmates. I still hold on to and continue to treasure some of those friendships today. Grades seven and eight and one grade nine class along with the principal's office and the gym were on the first floor of the school. The other two grade nine classes as well as grades ten, eleven, and twelve were upstairs, as were the library and the staff room. On stormy or very cold days, we usually stayed inside for our breaks. I can't recall when I first met or became acquainted with my brother's classmates, Stu and Wally. It seems to me that it was during some inclement weather that I first laid eyes on those legends in my mind. They usually spent their recesses and part of the lunch break standing in the doorway of their grade nine classroom upstairs where they would comment, snicker, and make intimidating remarks to or about girls who walked down the hallway.

The first time I walked past them, I smiled and said hi. Their snickering remarks to each other confused me. Clearly, they did not know the esteem I held for their humorous mischief. The next time I went by them, I smiled again. They were not friendly. In fact, I thought they were rude. I thought, "So, you're in grade nine. I'm not impressed!" I began paying closer attention and watching their behaviors toward other students, especially girls who walked past them in the hallway. These two sounded sexist and intimidating toward every female. I noticed some girls felt embarrassed, and some would make smart remarks back to them. That only served to up the ante.

The school year progressed, and by the time late Spring arrived, Wally and Stu, in my estimation, had fallen from legends to lizards, and I could walk by them without acknowledging their existence. I wasn't deaf though, and I could still hear their remarks about my clothing or my figure. One day as I walked past them, on my way to the library, and turned right at the end of the hallway, there was a group of girls congregating and seemed to be chatting about things they were afraid of. I knew some of the girls but not all of them. I smiled at them but did not disrupt their conversation as I walked around them. One girl, I didn't know, loudly proclaimed to another that she knew that Wally Wencel was scared to death of snakes. This was music to my ears. I stopped in my tracks and turned around to look at her. I wondered how she knew that but I didn't dare ask. My mind was already formulating its plan and I wasn't about to disclose it. I don't remember walking to the library. Perhaps I floated there. After all, it was Friday afternoon.

On Saturday, I found a large pickle bottle in the cellar way and punched a few holes in the lid using a nail and hammer. I sat it inside the back porch and filled it halfway with earth and grass. We had a few warm days and I was hopeful that I would find a snake. Last Fall, I had seen some so I knew they were around the yard and field. I didn't know how long I could keep one alive in the bottle so I decided to wait until Sunday to do my hunting.

Probably very few would describe catching snakes as 'a piece of cake' because they can be quick and slippery. But on my first attempt, I found a good-sized brown one, just over a foot long and as round as a nickel, in the field beside the house. I was happy and just wanted to get it safely into the jar. As I was about to go in through the back porch doorway, something moved on the grass to my right and caught my eye. Without hesitation, I grabbed it. It was a bright green Garter snake about nine inches long and not big around at all, maybe the diameter of a dime. The door wasn't latched and I kicked it open. I shoved both snakes inside that pickle jar and screwed the lid on. It felt like the universe was conspiring to help me and provided me with a snake for each one of them. I left the jar on a shelf inside the porch and sat a brown paper bag beside it to be ready for the morning when we would head to the bus stop together. I told no one what I was up to. I didn't want to hear from any naysayers especially when everything seemed to be presented to me and just falling into place. I fine-tuned my plan just before falling asleep.

Like everyone else at the bus stop, my arms were full of books, binders, and bags. When I boarded the bus, I sat the bag on the floor between my feet and unfolded the top. I held my books on my lap so as to not draw any attention or curiosity. When we got to school I went straight to my desk, once again unfolded the top of the bag, and put everything out of sight. I didn't know how long those snakes would live in that jar so I planned my surprise for recess, not lunchtime. When the bell rang, I grabbed the bag and went upstairs quickly and with purpose to the girl's washroom. It was located just slightly past and to the right of the grade nine room I would approach. As I hurried by, Wally and Stu had already taken their sentinel posts in the doorway. The washroom already seemed crowded, but I went straight to the first sink and opened the jar.

As I took the snakes out and held them in my hands, a few girls started screaming hysterically. It was as if one squeal had to be outdone by the other. I tried telling them, "They won't hurt you."

One screamed, "Let's go tell the teachers!" They swung the washroom door open and ran toward the staff room. I caught the door with my foot and went out behind them.

This was not part of my plan, but it couldn't have worked out better. Those screamers had caught the attention of Wally and Stu and, as they were looking toward the staff room to see what was happening, they didn't notice me walking across the hall toward them. It wasn't until I was standing directly and closely in front of them that they bothered to look at me. I wasted no time asking, "Hey, do you guys like snakes?" as I shoved a snake in each of their faces. I saw the blood drain and their faces go ashen. I also saw how they bumped into each other both trying to get back through the classroom door at the same time. They didn't fit side by side. I turned and hurried back toward the washroom, and out of the corner of my eye, I saw the teachers coming.

I had just put the snakes back into the jar and was screwing the lid on when the tattle-tales and two teachers entered. Mrs. Hennessy shouted, "Who has snakes in here?" As she looked at me she asked, "Do you have snakes?" She might have made a good lawyer because they only ask questions they already know the answer to; and besides, they had caught me with the evidence. In a moment like that, did they think I was stupid enough to lie? Mrs. Lamb chimed in saying I shouldn't bring snakes to school.

I asked them both, "Is there a rule that says I can't bring snakes to school?" I knew very well there was no such rule, but they weren't answering me. So, very politely, I kept asking, "Is there a rule? Am I breaking a rule?" Mrs. Lamb had chased the gloating girls out of the washroom and seemed to be trying hard to keep the smile off her face. Mrs. Hennessy, always composed and reasonable, explained to me that there was no rule, but I shouldn't bring snakes to school because they scare the other students. I thought to myself, *Precisely*! But I replied to her, "Then I'll take them outside and put them up at the end of the field." The teachers were satisfied with that. It didn't seem to be of interest as to why I brought the snakes to school and I wasn't telling. My mission was accomplished.

As I made my way across the field to release my assistants, my mind raced with thoughts of how those two boys could tease, taunt, intimidate, and verbally bully other students, especially girls, and get away with that behavior for almost a whole school year. Yet, there was a posse coming after me for bringing a couple of little snakes to school, and I wasn't trying to scare the girls with them, they were just too nosey. I guess the others weren't aware of it, but in my opinion, there were already a few snakes in that school. Mine were harmless, except they could, innocently, frighten cowards. It wasn't in the curriculum, but it was definitely a lesson those boys needed to learn before going into grade ten. That ain't no way to treat a lady; especially one with a jar of snakes. They both seemed to have learned their lesson well.

If anyone had told me then that I would one day marry one of those boys, I would have laughed and told them they were crazy. That would never happen! I have learned to never say never! It was a few years later and we were both at the same dance. Wally asked me to dance a few times with him, and I did. At the end of the evening, he asked if he could take me home. To my home, not his! I only lived across the road from the dancehall, and I still had a pretty good idea where the snakes were, so I said yes. For the next fifty years, he would bring joy, love, and laughter to my life.

It was a few years after we were married that I asked him if he remembered that day I held the snakes in front of his and Stu's faces. He looked at me with disdain in his eyes, and I detected a hint of shame directed toward me. With the emphasis on 'you', he said, "I can't believe that you did that."

I looked directly into his eyes and replied, "Believe it!"

Both of those boys, who were my grade eight legends and my grade nine lizards, grew up to be fine, respectable, and compassionate men. I like to think that snakes scared them onto a better path than the one they were traveling. When those snakes were introduced, there seemed to be an immediate and lasting behavioral change in those boys. Snakes may have taught them one of the most important lessons they learned in school.

Several years later I was working in the school system as a school psychologist. One day, I was asked to assess a six-year-old, grade one student. When I met with the classroom teacher, she gave me a little background on the child's non-compliant and disruptive behaviors at school as well as some information about his family situation. (I am quite certain she was unaware of my reputation or effectiveness with snakes.) No one was concerned with the intellectual abilities of this little boy but it was evident that his behaviors were interfering with his classroom learning and had become problematic for him and everyone else.

The teacher had escorted him to me in the room where I was to assess him. I wanted to get to know him and find out what he was interested in and what it was like to be him. We had only spent a few minutes together when he asked if he could go to the washroom. I let him go by himself. When he returned, I suggested we play a game. I wanted to interact with him and observe his strategies and how he handled winning and losing. He suggested we play X's and O's so that is what we did. His attention span was brief. I was always aware in these sessions that the child was evaluating me as much as I was him or her. After only a few games, many of which he won, the boy asked me, "Well, do you love me or do you hate me?"

Trying to hide my surprise, I said, "I don't know you very well yet." He repeated his question.

I asked, "Are these my only choices? I can love you or I can hate you?" He nodded yes and asked me again. He watched me as I purposely thought for a moment. Then I said, "Well, I don't hate you." I saw a trace of a smile, but he remained silent. He was probably thinking you will when I'm finished with you. I was thinking that how I answered his question was going to provide direction for him and his behaviors. It seemed he needed to take power in relationships, and I felt he only knew one way to do that. He had already checked me out to see how much leeway he had. If I hated him, he would ensure that continued; and if I loved him, he would work to change that as soon as possible. I sensed that love and hate were both experienced in the same way by him, amidst anger and punishment. Being hated would create a relationship stasis for him, while being loved meant he would have to be on his guard; keep his wits about him for when the shoe falls. Our time was almost up and I needed to walk him back to his classroom. I told him I'd be back next week to see him again, and we would spend some more time together. He seemed happy and in our relaxed one-on-one encounter, there were no problems.

When I returned to the school the following week, I was told the principal wanted to see me before I met with the student again. I knocked on her door. She asked me in and told me to have a seat on her sofa. I liked the pleasant, homey atmosphere of her office space. She said to me, "I understand you have already seen our little friend. Have you ever seen a kid like that before in your life?" I smiled and told her I had spent a little time with him last week and was just getting to know him. She said that his teacher sent him to her office the other day and when he came through the door, I told him to have a seat where you are seated now. Instead, he marched over to my bookcase here, with these books, ornaments, and pictures on it. She demonstrated with her right arm as she continued, "He took one swipe with his arm and knocked everything off the second shelf onto the floor. Then, he went and sat down."

She paused, and I continued to listen. She then said, "I didn't want to give him any reaction because that is what I figured he was looking for, so I just got up and went over there, bent over, and started picking up everything to put it back on the shelf." She added, "While I was bent over, I heard him say to me, 'You've got the biggest fuckin' ass I've ever seen'!" She said, "I couldn't stand up right away because I was laughing so hard. I had to stay there, bent over until I could gain my composure." The principal wanted to let me know how incorrigible this six-year-old was, perhaps so I could be better prepared for him than she had been.

I told her I wanted to meet with his mother and grandmother who were his primary caregivers. I was told to set up the meeting soon because the mother had been accepted into the military and was leaving for boot camp in a week or so. Apparently, after the father had abandoned them, the mother and child had to move in with her mother. They were struggling financially and the boy's mother needed a sustainable income. It was decided she would join the military and her mother would care for the child while she was away. The boy had no say in the changes that had happened and were continuing to happen in his life. The adults were distraught and had no time or skills to cope with the angry, purposeful, and out-of-control behaviors he exhibited to show them his hurt, his needs, and his disapproval.

As I left the office to go make a call to the boy's mom, I considered how the principal didn't want to 'give him any reaction,' but of course, she did. More important was how the child interpreted the reaction she gave to him. From what I had already learned about him, I could only imagine what he must have been thinking and feeling. Probably things like: Your stuff means more to you than I do; you don't care if I'm being punished or angry, you don't care what happened to me today, you are just going to ignore me and leave me alone. Well, I'll show you!

At least that is what I thought might have gone through my little six-year-old mind if I was in his shoes. With every inappropriate action and boundary crossing, a little child is really saying, "Can you hear me now?" "Can you hear my voice this time?" If as adults, we don't ever hear them; or if we do and continuously ignore them, we are not teaching problem-solving. We are simply reinforcing what they already believe: They don't matter. Every time a child performs an obnoxious behavior, it is the child screaming, "I do matter!" Don't they have a right to expect adults to listen, to hear them, to teach them a better way instead of just punishing them? They don't know better, but we do.

We can't pretend five and six-year-olds don't have a history. They do. And they enter school with all the information and learning they have acquired. Don't bother checking the backpack. It's not there. But rest assured, the little ones will show us what they have learned and what they believe. Teachers prefer a clean slate, but it is only the parents who get the Tabula Rasa. Teachers have to begin their instructions in the child's history class, and sometimes it requires what they are not trained to do: Unteach.

How does a child, or any of us for that matter, unlearn what we know? We don't. It's all there consciously or unconsciously. But we can learn new things, and new behaviors and, if consistent, we may find those new behaviors work better for us in life. That's a lesson we can all learn and benefit from learning.